He *guessed* what *she wanted to hear first*

"Your cats are with my housekeeper, happy and safe." He paused while a large pot of tea was put before her. It looked heaven-sent, but she didn't take her eyes off his face.

"If you would consider it, there is a job waiting for you. The pay is small, but you'll be fed and housed."

"Well," said Henrietta, and took a sip of tea. "I thought that you had said things you hadn't meant just to be rid of me, but it's not like that at all. I have been thinking awful things about you, and all the time you've been kind and helpful and there was no need—you don't even know me.... I'm very grateful."

Mr. Ross-Pitt concealed his feelings admirably. "Be brave, Henrietta. Burn your boats."

She smiled then—she had a lovely smile, lighting up her whole face. "Yes, all right, I will."

Betty Neels spent her childhood and youth in Devonshire, England, before training as a nurse and midwife. She was an army nursing sister during the war, married a Dutchman and subsequently lived in Holland for fourteen years. She lives with her husband in Dorset, and has a daughter and a grandson. Her hobbies are reading, animals—she owns two cats—old buildings and writing. Betty began to write on retirement from nursing, incited by a lady in a library bemoaning the lack of romance novels.

Books by Betty Neels

HARLEQUIN ROMANCE®
3467—THE RIGHT KIND OF GIRL
3492—MARRYING MARY
3512—A KISS FOR JULIE
3527—THE VICAR'S DAUGHTER

Don't miss any of our special offers. Write to us at the following address for information on our newest releases.

Harlequin Reader Service
U.S.: 3010 Walden Ave., P.O. Box 1325, Buffalo, NY 14269
Canadian: P.O. Box 609, Fort Erie, Ont. L2A 5X3

$\mathcal{B}$etty Neels
Only By Chance

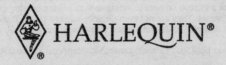

HARLEQUIN®

TORONTO • NEW YORK • LONDON
AMSTERDAM • PARIS • SYDNEY • HAMBURG
STOCKHOLM • ATHENS • TOKYO • MILAN • MADRID
PRAGUE • WARSAW • BUDAPEST • AUCKLAND

ISBN 0-373-03537-3

ONLY BY CHANCE

First North American Publication 1999.

Copyright © 1996 by Betty Neels.

Printed in U.S.A.

CHAPTER ONE

IT WAS Monday morning and the occupational therapy department at St Alkelda's Hospital was filling up fast.

Not only were patients being trundled from the wards to spend a few hours painting and knitting, making paper chains ready for a distant Christmas, learning to use their hands and brains once again, but ambulances were depositing outpatients in a steady flow, so that the staff had their work cut out sorting them out and taking them to wherever they were to spend the morning.

The occupational therapist was a large, severe-looking woman, excellent at her job but heartily disliked by those who worked for her, for she had an overbearing manner and a sarcastic tongue, always ready to find fault but rarely to praise. She was finding fault now with a girl half her size, with an unassuming face, mousy hair and a tendency to slight plumpness.

'Must you be so slow, Henrietta? Really, you are of little use to me unless you can make more of an effort.'

The girl paused, an elderly lady on either arm. She said in a reasonable voice, 'Neither Mrs Flood nor Miss Thomas can hurry, Mrs Carter. That's why I'm slow.'

Mrs Carter looked daggers, but, before she could think up something to squash this perfectly sensible remark, Henrietta had hoisted the elderlies more firmly onto their feet and was making for the room where the paper chains were being made.

Mrs Carter stared after the trio. Really, the girl was impossible, making remarks like that, and always politely and in a tiresomely matter-of-fact voice which it was impossible to complain about.

Not even trained, Henrietta was a mere part-timer, dealing with the more mundane tasks which the qualified staff had no time for—helping the more helpless of the patients to eat their dinner, escorting them to the ambulances, setting them in their chairs, finding mislaid spectacles, and, when she wasn't doing that, showing them how to make paper flowers, unravelling their knitting, patiently coaxing stiff, elderly fingers to hold a paintbrush.

Doing everything cheerfully and willingly, thought Mrs Carter crossly. The girl's too good to be true.

Henrietta, aware that Mrs Carter disliked her and would have liked to get rid of her if possible, was glad when her day's work ended.

The last of the elderlies safely stowed in the last ambulance, she began to tidy the place ready for the next day, thankful that she wouldn't be there tomorrow. Three days a week was all that was required of her, and although it was hard to make ends meet on her wages she was glad to have the job, even though there was no guarantee of its permanence.

The last to leave, she locked the doors, took the keys along to the porter's office and went out into the cold dark of a January evening. The side-door she used opened out of one side of the hospital, and she began walking over this deserted area towards the lighted forecourt, only to stop halfway there, arrested by a very small mewing sound. It came from a tiny kitten, wobbling unsteadily towards her, falling over itself in its anxiety to reach her.

Henrietta got down on her knees, the better to see the small creature. 'Lost?' she asked it, and then added, 'Starved and dirty and very frightened.' She picked it up and felt its bird-like bones under the dirty fur. 'Well, I'm not leaving you here; you can come home with me.' She rocked back on her heels, stood up, stepped backwards and discovered that she was standing on a foot.

'Whoops,' said Henrietta, and spun round. 'So sorry...' She found herself addressing a waistcoat, and looked higher to glimpse its owner—a large, tall man, peering down at her. Not that he could see much of her in the gloom, nor, for that matter, could she see much of him. 'It's a kitten,' she explained. 'It's lost and so very thin.'

The man put out a hand and took the little animal from her. 'Quite right; he or she needs a home without a doubt.'

'Oh, that's easy; he or she can come home with me.' She took the kitten back. 'I hope I didn't hurt your foot?' When he didn't answer she added, 'Goodnight.'

He watched her go, wondering who she was and what she was doing there. Not one of the nurses, he supposed, although he hadn't been able to see her very clearly. He would remember her voice, though, quiet and pleasant—serene was the word he sought for and found.

Henrietta tucked the kitten inside her coat and walked home. Home was a bedsitting room in a tall, shabby old house ten minutes away from the hospital. There was nothing fashionable about that part of London, but for the most part it was respectable, the houses which lined the streets mostly divided into flats or bedsitters. It was lonely too, for its inhabitants kept themselves very much to themselves, passing each other with only a brief nod, intent on minding their own business.

Henrietta mounted the steps to the front door, entered and went up the staircase in the narrow hall to the top floor, where she unlocked her own door. It opened directly into a large attic room with small windows at each end of it. A large, rather battered tabby-cat got off the window-sill of the back window and came to meet her.

'Dickens, hello.' She bent to stroke his elderly coat. 'You want your supper, don't you? And we've got ourselves a companion, so be nice to him or her.'

She put the scrap down on the shabby rug before an old-fashioned gas fire. Dickens first backed away and then began to examine the kitten. He was still sniffing cautiously when she went back with his supper, turned on the fire and fetched a towel to clean some of the dirt off the kitten. Then she offered it a saucer of warm milk, which it licked slowly at first and then with speed.

'There's plenty more,' said Henrietta, and went to hang her coat behind the curtain screening off the far end of the room. There was a divan bed there too, with a bedside table, and under the front window another table covered with an old-fashioned chenille cloth.

There was a small easy chair, two wooden chairs at the table and another basket chair enlivened by a bright cushion. Nothing matched; they looked as though they had come from an Oxfam shop, or one of the second-hand shops close by. As indeed they had.

Still, it was home to Henrietta, and it had certain advantages. Beyond the back window there was a small balcony, sufficient for Dickens's needs, and she had a pot of catmint there, another of grass, and a cut-down branch which she had tied to the iron railing surrounding the balcony so that he could sharpen his claws. In the spring she planted daffodils in an old broken-down earthen pot which she had found unused in the back garden of the house.

She had been there for a couple of years now, and as far as she could see she had little chance of finding something more congenial. Rents, even in that shabby-genteel part of London, were high, and it was an effort to make ends meet. Her hospital job barely covered the rent, gas, electricity, and the most basic of food, and she relied on her other job to keep the wolf from the door.

Each morning she left the house just after six o'clock, took a bus to the block of offices a mile away and joined a team of cleaners, working until half past eight and then going home again. On the days she worked at the hospital it was rather a rush, but she worked there from ten o'clock until the late afternoon, and so far she had managed to get there on time.

Her days were full and sometimes tiring but, despite her smallness, she was strong and healthy and possessed of a cheerful disposition, and if at times she thought with longing of a home life and a family she didn't dwell on them.

She couldn't remember her father or mother; they had both died in an air disaster when she had been no more than a year or so old. She had been left with her grandparents while her mother—their daughter—had accompanied her father on a business trip to South America, and, since they had stubbornly refused to countenance her marriage and had agreed only with great reluctance to look after their small granddaughter, any affection they might have felt for Henrietta had been swallowed up in resentment and anger at their daughter's death.

A nursemaid had been found for her and she had seen very little of her grandparents. When her grandmother died, her grandfather had declared that he was quite unable to care for her and, since there had been no relations willing to have her, Henrietta had been sent to a children's home.

She had been almost six years old then. She'd stayed until she was eighteen and, since it had been a well-run institution and the supervisor a kind and intelligent woman, Henrietta had taken her A levels and stayed on for three more years, teaching the little ones and making herself useful. It had been a restricted life, but the only one she'd known, and she'd been tolerably happy.

Then the supervisor had retired and her successor had been able to see no point in keeping Henrietta there. She had been told that she might go out into the world and earn her living like everyone else. 'You can teach,' she'd been told. 'There are plenty of jobs if you look for them.'

So she'd left the place that she had regarded as home for almost all her life and, armed with the small amount of money that she had been given to tide her over, she'd gone looking for work. In this she had been lucky for the first job she'd gone after—office cleaner—had been hers for the asking.

She'd taken it and, helped by one of the other cleaners, had rented this attic room, eking out her wages with her tiny capital, taking on any job to keep her going— serving at a stall at the market on Saturday afternoons, babysitting for her landlady's daughter, distributing circulars. Bit by bit she'd furnished her room, and, since she had a nice dress sense, had acquired a small wardrobe from Oxfam. She'd acquired Dickens, too...

Things had looked up; she'd answered an advertisement for an assistant at the occupational therapy department at the hospital only a few streets away, and she had been there for more than a year now. There was always the hope that one or other of the full-time workers would leave and she would be able to apply for the job.

She took another look at the kitten, wrapped in an old scarf, and left it to sleep, watched by Dickens, while she got her supper.

Later, when she turned the divan into a bed ready to get into it, she lifted the kitten onto the end where

Dickens had already curled up. It made a brave effort to purr, scoffed some bread and milk and fell asleep, and Dickens, who had a kind heart under his ferocious appearance, edged closer so that the small creature could feel his warm and furry body.

Henrietta got into bed. 'You're a splendid fellow, Dickens,' she told him as she put out the light and heard his raucous purr.

She had to be up early, of course, but once she was dressed and on her way even on a miserably cold and dark morning it wasn't too bad. She would go home presently, and have breakfast and do her small chores, initiate the kitten into the pleasures of the balcony and do her careful shopping.

The other cleaners greeted her cheerfully as they started their work but there wasn't time to gossip, and once they had finished they wasted no time in getting back home. Henrietta, standing on a crowded bus, thought of her breakfast—toast and a boiled egg and a great pot of tea...

The cats were still on the bed, but they got down as she went in. She lighted the fire and, since the room was cold, gave them their breakfasts and fetched the cardboard box lined with old blanket that Dickens regarded as his own. She watched while he got in, to sit washing his face after his meal, and presently, when the kitten crept in beside him, he took no notice. Then, his own toilet completed, he began to clean the kitten and, that done to his satisfaction, they both went to sleep again.

Henrietta, lingering over her own breakfast, was doing her weekly sums. Each week she managed to save something—never very much, but even the coppers and the small silver mounted up slowly in the jamjar on the shelf beside the gas stove in one corner of the room. It was a flimsy shield against the ever present threat of being out of work.

Presently she tidied up, got into a coat, tied a scarf over her head and went to the shops, where she laid out her money with a careful eye. Since the shopkeepers in the neighbourhood liked her, because she never asked for credit, the butcher gave her a marrowbone to add to the stewing steak she had bought, and the baker threw in a couple of rolls with the yesterday's loaf she bought.

She bore her purchases home, fed the cat and kitten, ate her snack lunch and set about cleaning the room. It didn't take long, so that presently she drew the armchair up to the fire and opened her library book, waiting patiently while Dickens made himself comfortable on her lap.

When he had settled she lifted the kitten on too, and he made room for it, rumbling in his hoarse voice in what she hoped was a fatherly fashion. Apparently it was, for the kitten curled up as close as it could get and went to sleep at once.

Henrietta worked at St Alkelda's on Monday, Wednesday and Thursday of each week and did her cleaning on each weekday morning—a monotonous round of dull days enlivened by her free Sundays, when she took herself off to one of London's parks and then went to evensong at any one of London's churches. She was by no means content with her lot, but she didn't grumble; she had work and a roof over her head, and things would get better.

She was saving every penny so that she could enrol at night school and learn shorthand and typing. The course didn't cost much, but it meant bus fares, notebooks, pens and pencils, and perhaps hidden extras that she knew nothing about. Besides, she needed to have money to fall back on should she find herself out of work. She had as much chance of being made redundant as anyone else.

It was a good thing that the owner of the fruit and vegetable stall at Saturday's market had taken her on in the afternoon. He paid very little, but she didn't blame him for that—he had to live as well—and he allowed her to take home a cauliflower or a bag of apples by way of perks. The jamjar was filling up nicely—another six months or so and she could start on plans to improve things.

'A pity you haven't any looks worth mentioning,' she told the looking-glass hanging above the rickety chest of drawers. 'No one—that is, to speak plainly, no *man*—is going to look at you twice and whisk you off to the altar. You have to become a career girl, so that by the time you're thirty you'll be carrying one of those briefcases and wearing a tailored suit and high heels.' She nodded at her reflection.

Later, as she gave Dickens and the kitten their suppers, she uttered aloud a thought which had been at the back of her head for quite some time. 'I wonder who he was—the man whose foot I trod upon? He had a nice voice...'

Dickens paused in his gobbling to give her a thoughtful look, but the kitten didn't want to waste time—he ate up and then mewed for more.

'I shall call you Oliver Twist; you're always asking for second helpings,' said Henrietta, filling his saucer. So the kitten acquired a name twice as big as itself which inevitably within a few hours had been shortened to Ollie.

She heard the voice again on the following Monday afternoon, towards the end of a tiring day, and most unfortunately she was quite unable to turn round and see its owner. She was sitting facing the wall between two old ladies who, what with having trouble with their dentures and shaking hands, needed a good deal of help with the tea and buns they were enjoying.

If there had been no one else there, Henrietta would have turned round and taken a look, but Mrs Carter was with him, droning on about something or other; she was always complaining bitterly to any of the medical staff who might have come to the department to see how a patient was getting on.

The owner of the voice was listening patiently, his eyes on the back of Henrietta's mousy bun of hair, recognising her at once—which upon reflection surprised him, for he hadn't seen her clearly. Perhaps it was her voice, quiet and cheerful, urging the old ladies to enjoy their tea.

Mrs Carter paused for breath and he said, 'Yes, indeed, Mrs Carter,' which encouraged her to start again as he allowed his thoughts to wander. Not that he allowed that to show. His handsome face was wearing the bland listening expression he so often hid behind when he was with someone he disliked, and he disliked Mrs Carter. She was efficient, ran her department on oiled wheels, but he had upon occasion seen how she treated her staff... He became aware of what Mrs Carter was saying.

'I need more trained staff, sir. I'm fobbed off with anyone who chooses to apply for a job here. That girl there, sitting between those two patients—she does her best but she's not carrying her weight, and when she's reproved she answers back. No manners, but what can you expect these days? She'll have to go, of course.'

She had made no effort to lower her rather loud voice and the man beside her frowned. It was obvious that the girl had heard every word; probably she had been meant to.

He said clearly, 'It appears to me that she is coping admirably, Mrs Carter. One does not need to be highly skilled to be patient and kind, and the young lady you mention appears to possess both these virtues...'

Mrs Carter bridled. 'Well, I'm sure you are right, sir.' She would have liked to argue about it, but although she would never admit it, even to herself, she was a little in awe of him.

He was a senior consultant—she had heard him described as a medical genius—who specialised in brain surgery. He was a giant of a man with more than his share of good looks and, it was said, the world's goods. Not that anyone knew for certain; he rarely spoke about himself to his colleagues, and if they knew about his private life they never spoke of it.

He said now, 'I should like to take a look at Mrs Collins. Is she making any progress? There was a certain lack of co-ordination after I operated, but there should be some improvement.'

Henrietta heard Mrs Carter answer as they walked away, but she still didn't turn round. She knew who he was now; at least, she knew that he was someone important in the hospital. He had put Mrs Carter neatly in her place, and Henrietta was grateful for his kindness, but she hoped that she would never meet him face to face—she would die of shame...

As usual she was the last to leave. She locked up and hurried across to the porter's office to hand over the keys. It was another dark and wet evening, and she couldn't wait to get home and have a cup of tea. Mrs Carter's remarks had worried her; she didn't think that she would be sacked unless she had done something truly awful, and although Mrs Carter was always finding fault she had never threatened her with dismissal.

She bade the porter goodnight and made her way to

the side-door, ducking her head at the sudden gust of wind and rain until brought to a sudden halt by something solid. An arm steadied her.

'Ah, I was afraid that I might have missed you. I feel that I owe you an apology on Mrs Carter's behalf. But let us be more comfortable in the car while I give it.'

'I'm going home,' said Henrietta, 'and there is really no need...'

She could have saved her breath. The arm, solid as a rock but gentle, was urging her across the forecourt to the sacred corner where the consultants parked their cars. Her companion opened the door of one of them—a Bentley—popped her inside, got in his side and turned to her. 'That's better. What is your name?'

Was he going to give her the sack? she thought wildly. She had been told that the consultants had a good deal of influence. She sat up straight, her nose twitching at the faint whiff of good leather upholstery. 'Henrietta Cowper.'

He offered a large hand. 'Ross-Pitt.'

She shook it. 'How do you do, Mr Ross-Pitt?'

She gave him an enquiring look and he said at once, 'You will have heard every word Mrs Carter uttered this afternoon. I can assure you that there have been no complaints about your work. Mrs Carter is an excellent organiser, and knows her job inside out, but she can be rather hard on people. I'm sure she didn't mean all she said!'

Henrietta, who knew better, didn't contradict him and he went on, 'You like your work?' His voice was friendly but detached.

'Yes, thank you.'

'You're not full-time?'

'No, no, three days a week.' She paused. 'It is kind

of you to explain, Mr Ross-Pitt. I'm grateful.' She put a hand on the door. 'Goodbye.'

'I'll drive you home. Stay where you are; it's pelting down—you'll drown.'

'I live very near here...'

The engine was purring almost silently. 'Where?'

'Well, Denvers Street; it's a turning off the main road on the left-hand side, but there's no need...'

He took no notice of that, but drove out of the forecourt into the busy main road. 'The third turning on the left,' said Henrietta, and then added, 'It's number thirty, halfway down on the right.'

When he stopped she started to scramble out, only to be restrained by his hand. 'Wait.' He had a very quiet voice. 'Have you a key?'

'The door isn't locked; it's flatlets and bedsitters.'

He got out and opened her door, and waited while she got out. 'Thank you very much.' She looked up into his placid face. 'Do get back into your car; you'll get soaked.' She smiled at him. 'Goodnight, sir.'

He gave a little nod. 'Goodnight, Miss Henrietta Cowper.' He waited in the rain until she had gone into the house.

A funny little thing, he reflected as he drove away. Lovely eyes, but an ordinary face. Of course, wet hair hanging around a rain-washed face hardly helped. He liked her voice, though. He turned the car and drove back to the main road, making for the motorway which would take him to his home.

He had a flat above his consulting rooms in Wimpole Street, but home was a rambling old house just south of Thaxted, and since the hospital was close to the M11 he chose to travel to and fro. After a day in the operating theatre or a session in Outpatients he enjoyed the drive, and the drive to the city in the early morning, even in mid-winter, was no problem—the Bentley swallowed the miles with well-bred silent speed while he considered the day's work ahead of him.

He joined the motorway and sat back, relaxed behind the wheel, reviewing several of his patients' progress, weighing the pros and cons of each case and, that done, allowed his thoughts to roam.

Miss Henrietta Cowper, he reflected, at first glance was a nonentity, but he suspected that there was more to her than that. A square peg in a round hole, perhaps? Was there an intelligent brain behind that small, plain face? He thought that there was. Mrs Carter had seen that and resented it.

So why didn't the girl train as a nurse, or, for that matter, go into computers or something similar? Her home had looked shabby from the outside, but the street was a quiet well-kept one, despite it being in one of the East End's run-down areas.

He turned the car off the motorway and drove for another ten minutes or so along a country road, until he slowed between a handful of cottages and turned again past the church, up the main street of the village and then through his own gates. The drive was short, widening out before the front of the house. He got out and stood a moment looking at it—white walls, half-timbered, with a tiled roof, charming lattice windows, glowing with lamplight, a porch and a solid wood door.

Its Tudor origins were apparent, although since then it had been added to from time to time, but nothing had been changed during the last two hundred years. It stood overlooking the wintry garden, offering a warm welcome, and when the door was opened a Labrador dog galloped out to greet him.

Mr Ross-Pitt bent to greet the eager beast. 'Watson, old fellow—wanting a walk? Presently.'

They went in together to be greeted by his housekeeper. Mrs Patch was elderly, stout and good-natured. She ran his home beautifully, with the help of a girl from the village and Mrs Lock, who came to do the rough work twice a week. She said comfortably, 'There you are, sir. I've just this minute taken a batch of scones out of the oven—just right for your tea.'

He put a hand on her plump shoulder. 'Mrs Patch, you're a treasure; I'm famished. Give me five minutes...' He went along a short passage leading from the roomy square hall and opened the door at its end.

His study was at the side of the house, its French doors opening onto the garden. Now its crimson velvet curtains were closed against the dark night and a fire burned briskly in the steel grate. He sat down at his desk, put his bag beside his chair and turned on the answering machine. Most of the messages were unimportant, and several were from friends—they could be dealt with later.

He left the room and crossed the hall to the drawing room—an irregular-shaped room with windows on two sides, an inglenook and a ceiling which exhibited its original strapwork.

The furniture was a pleasing mixture of comfortable armchairs and sofas, lamp-tables placed where they were most needed, and a bow-fronted cabinet which took up almost all of one wall. It was filled with porcelain and silver, handed down from one generation to the next. He remembered how as a small boy his grandmother had allowed him to hold some of the figurines in his hands.

He had inherited the house from her, and had altered nothing save to have some unobtrusive modernising of the kitchen. He disliked central heating, but the house

was warm; the Aga in the kitchen never went out and
there were fires laid in every room, ready to be lighted.

He went to his chair near the fire and Mrs Patch followed him in with the tea-tray.

'It's no night to be out in,' she observed, setting the
tray down on a table at his elbow, 'nor yet to be in a
miserable cold room somewhere. I pity those poor souls
living in bedsitting rooms.'

Was Henrietta Cowper living like that? he wondered.

Each week he spent an evening at a clinic in Stepney;
only the two young doctors who ran it knew who he was
and he never talked about it.

It had given him an insight into the lives of most of
the patients—unemployed for the most part, in small,
half-furnished rooms with not enough warmth or light.

On occasion he had needed to go and see them in
their homes and he had done what he could, financing
the renting of an empty shop where volunteers offered
tea and soup and loaves. No one knew about this and
he never intended that they should...

Presently he got into his coat again and took Watson
for his evening walk. It was still raining and very dark,
but he had known the country around his home since
he'd been a small boy; he followed well-remembered
lanes with Watson trotting beside him. The country,
even on a night such as this, was vastly better than London streets.

If, during the following week, Mr Ross-Pitt thought of
Henrietta at all it was briefly; his days were full, his
leisure largely filled too. He rode whenever he could,
and was much in demand at his friends' and acquaintances' dinner tables, for he was liked by everyone, un-
failingly good-natured and placid. Too placid, some of

his women-friends thought; a delightful companion, but never showing the least desire to fall in love.

It was on the next Monday morning that he went down to the occupational therapy unit to check on a patient's progress since he had operated on him to remove a brain tumour. His progress was excellent, and he told Mrs Carter so.

'Well, I'm sure we do our best, sir, although it's hard going—there's that girl, not turned up this morning. I knew she would be no good when she was taken on—'

'Perhaps she is ill?'

'Ill?' Mrs Carter snorted in disgust. 'These young women don't know the meaning of a good day's work, she'll turn up on Wednesday with some excuse.'

He answered rather absent-mindedly and presently went away, his mind already engrossed with the patient he was to see that afternoon—a difficult case which would need all his skill.

It was on Wednesday evening that he went along to the clinic, after being at the hospital for most of the day. It was another wet night, cold and windy with a forecast of snow, and the dark streets were gloomy. There was a light over the clinic door, dispelling some of the dreariness.

He parked the car and went inside, past the crowd in the waiting room, to the two small rooms at the back. Both doctors were already there. He greeted them cheerfully, threw his coat onto a chair and put on his white coat.

'A full house,' he observed. 'Is there anyone you want me to see?'

'Old Mr Wilkins is back again—blood pressure up, headaches, feels giddy...'

Mr Ross-Pitt nodded. 'I'll take a look.' He went into

the second room, cast his eye over Mr Wilkins' notes and then fetched him from the waiting room. After that he worked without pause; the clinic was supposed to shut at eight o'clock, but it never did. As long as there was a patient waiting it remained open, and that evening it was busier than usual.

It was almost nine o'clock when the younger of the two doctors put his head round the door. 'Could you cast an eye over this girl? She's just been brought in—came in a greengrocer's van. Looks ill. Not our usual type of patient, though; ought to have gone to her own doctor.'

'Let's have a look…' Mr Ross-Pitt went into the almost empty waiting room.

His eye passed over the two elderly women who came regularly, not because they were ill but because it was warm and cheerful; they were the first to arrive and the last to leave. It passed over the young man waiting for his girlfriend, who was with the other doctor, and lighted on the small group on the bench nearest the door—a shabby young man with a kind face and an elderly woman with beady black eyes, and between them, propped up, was Henrietta, looking very much the worse for wear.

Mr Ross-Pitt bit back the words on his tongue and went to bend over her.

'Miss Cowper, can you tell me what happened?'

She lifted her head and looked at him hazily. 'I'm not feeling well,' she said unhelpfully, and the woman spoke up.

'Bin ill since Saturday night—got a room at my 'ouse, yer see—never see 'er on Monday and Tuesday, and then she went to work this morning same as usual and they brought 'er back. Fainted all over the place, she did.'

He frowned. Why hadn't they kept her at the hospital if she had been taken ill there? His thought was answered before he could utter it. 'They couldn't bring her back at once, see? They 'as ter get the offices cleaned before eight o'clock, and someone 'ad ter finish 'er jobs for 'er.'

'Yes, yes. How far away is this job? How was she brought home?'

'On a bus, o' course; there ain't no money for taxis for the likes of us. Put 'er ter bed, I did; leastways, got 'er ter lie down and put a blanket over 'er. Thought she'd pick up, but she ain't much better.'

'You didn't take her to the hospital?'

'Brought 'er 'ere, 'aven't we?'

'You have done quite right. I'd like to see her in the surgery, please.'

He scooped Henrietta up, nodded to the woman to come too, and carried her to the second empty room.

Ten minutes later he sat down at the desk to write up his notes while Henrietta was wrapped up in her elderly coat and a scarf was tied over her head.

'A rather nasty influenza,' said Mr Ross-Pitt. 'She'll be all right in a few days, provided she takes these tablets regularly, stays in bed and keeps warm.'

Henrietta opened her eyes, then. 'I'm never ill; I'll be all right at home.'

'You'll look after her?' asked Mr Ross-Pitt, taking no notice of this. 'She should have gone to her own doctor, you know.'

'Couldn't, could she? He don't see no one on a Sunday, unless they're at their last gasp, and on weekdays she 'as ter be at the offices by half past six.'

'In the morning?'

'O' course. Them clerks and posh businessmen don't want no cleaning ladies mopping floors round 'em, do they?' She gave him a pitying look. 'Don't know much, do yer?'

Mr Ross-Pitt took this in good part. 'I'm learning,' he observed placidly, and smiled so that the woman smiled too.

'I dare say you're a good doctor,' she conceded. 'We'll get 'er back 'ome.'

'I have a car outside. Supposing I drive Miss Cowper back and you go ahead and get her bed ready and the room warm?'

'If yer say so.'

Henrietta opened an eye. 'I'm quite able to manage on my own.' She added with weary politeness, 'Thank you.'

He quite rightly ignored this remark too, and, since she felt too peculiar to protest, he carried her out to his car after a brief word with his two colleagues, laid her gently on the back seat and followed the greengrocer's van through the murky night. Henrietta, her eyes tight shut against a ferocious headache, said crossly, 'I'm perfectly all right.'

'Close your eyes and be quiet,' said Mr Ross-Pitt. 'You aren't going to be all right for a couple of days, but you'll feel better once you're snug in bed.'

Henrietta made a half-hearted sound which sounded like 'pooh' and slid back into uneasy dozing. She really was too weary to bother.

CHAPTER TWO

MR. ROSS-PITT slid to a gentle halt behind the van and got out of his car to find the van's owner waiting for him. 'Mrs Gregg's gone up ter see ter the room,' he explained. 'Do you want an 'and?'

'I think I can manage. The room is upstairs?'

'Top of the 'ouse, mate. Bit of a climb, but she's not all that 'eavy.' He grinned. 'And yer no lightweight.'

Mr Ross-Pitt smiled. 'I'll carry Miss Cowper upstairs. Thanks for your help—quick thinking on your part to bring her to the clinic.'

'My old lady's been on and off. Thinks 'ighly of it.'

'Thank you.' Mr Ross-Pitt opened the door of the car and lifted Henrietta out.

She roused herself from a feverish doze to protest. 'I'm very comfortable, thank you, if I could just go to sleep...'

Mr Ross-Pitt trod up the narrow stairs, his magnificent nose flaring at the all-pervading smell of cabbage, cooked to its death, mingled with a strong whiff of onions. By the time he reached the top floor the smell was fainter, but it was a good deal colder and the room he entered, the door obligingly left open by the landlady, was icy.

'I've lit the fire,' Mrs Gregg told him unnecessarily. She was smoothing the rumpled bed and shaking out Henrietta's nightgown—a sensible garment chosen for its warmth rather than its glamour.

He took a quick look round the room, laid Henrietta on the bed, and said, 'I'll be outside on the landing. I'll

take another look at Miss Cowper when you've put her
to bed.'

He paused as he went to the door. Sitting in his cardboard box, Dickens was glaring at him, the kitten huddled against him. 'Well, well,' said Mr Ross-Pitt, and
went downstairs to find the van driver.

'Will there be a shop open?' he wanted to know.
'Miss Cowper will need milk and eggs, some kind of
cold drink, and there are two cats which will need to be
fed.'

'Two now, is it? Me shop's shut, but I'll bring what
you want for her—I'm in the next street.'

Mr Ross-Pitt produced money. 'That's good of you. I
take it Miss Cowper is on her own?'

'Yes—'as been ever since she came 'ere. And as nice
a young lady as you could find in a month of Sundays.
Never says nothing about 'erself, though. Proper lady
she is, too. I'll be off. Bring it upstairs, shall I?'

'Please.' Mr Ross-Pitt went back upstairs, knocked on
the door and was admitted. Henrietta was in her bed.
Her appearance reminded him of a wet hen, and he studied her with no more than a professional eye. She was
flushed and hot, and her hair, of which there seemed to
be a great quantity, covered the pillow.

He took her wrist and frowned over her rapid pulse.
If he had known that she lived in an attic with, as far as
he could see, few comforts, he would have driven her to
St Alkelda's and had her admitted. She opened her eyes
and he said kindly, 'You're back in your bed. Stay there
for a couple of days and take the pills I'm going to leave
with you.'

'Dickens,' she whispered from a sore throat, 'and
Ollie. Don't let them out.'

'No, no, they are sitting in a box. I'll feed them before
I go; that's what you want, isn't it?'

She nodded. 'Please.' She turned her head and saw Mrs Gregg on the other side of the bed. 'Sorry to be such a nuisance...' She added anxiously, 'Don't let them out...'

Mr Ross-Pitt took her hand. 'I promise you your cats will be taken care of until you feel better. Mrs Gregg is going to keep an eye on you and them, and someone will be along to see how you feel tomorrow.'

There was a knock on the door and the milk and groceries were handed in. Mr Ross-Pitt took them, refusing to accept the change with exactly the right casual air. 'Certainly not, my dear chap; we're beholden to you.'

'Oh, I'll nip off 'ome then; the missus will be wondering where I've got to. So long, guv.'

'So long.' Mr Ross-Pitt went back into the room and stowed everything away tidily, fed the animals and then thoughtfully put them on the end of the bed. Henrietta didn't open her eyes but he saw her little smile.

'Will you leave a small light on, Mrs Gregg? Perhaps we might have a word downstairs.'

The word, accompanied by the handing-over of suitable financial support, didn't take long. 'Miss Cowper should be in hospital, but I am sure that you will take good care of her. Someone will visit her tomorrow to make sure that she is quite comfortable, but I know I can depend on you, Mrs Gregg.'

Mrs Gregg fingered the notes in her pocket and assured him that she would look after Henrietta like a mother.

Which she did. She wasn't one to bother about her various tenants—as long as they paid their rent and kept quite quiet she felt no concern for them—but Henrietta was a good tenant, paid her rent on the dot and was as quiet as a mouse. No gentlemen-friends, either. Mrs

Gregg would have done her best for her even without being paid for it.

As it was, she rose to the occasion, going upstairs several times during the night and following morning, warming milk, offering cold drinks, feeding the cat and kitten. She washed Henrietta's face and hands and straightened the bed while Henrietta tottered, wrapped in her dressing gown, down to the floor below to the loo, where she was quietly sick, to return, very wobbly on her feet, and climb thankfully back into bed.

The doctor with whom she had registered came to see her later that day. He was a busy man with a large practice but, asked courteously by Mr Ross-Pitt to visit Henrietta, he had consented to do so. He had agreed, too, to let him know if she showed signs of improvement.

He had been taken aback at the sight of the attic; she had been to his surgery once or twice and he had formed the vague opinion that she was a cut above his usual patient, probably living in one of the new blocks of flats springing up on the bulldozed sites of abandoned terraced houses.

He examined her carefully, wondering why Mr Ross-Pitt, whom he had met once or twice at the hospital, should take an interest in her. He had said something about her working at St Alkelda's, which would account for it, he supposed.

He phoned the hospital later and, since Mr Ross-Pitt wasn't available, he left a message. Miss Cowper was suffering from flu and not feeling too good, but she seemed a sensible young woman, taking her antibiotics and staying in bed, and her landlady appeared to be a good sort.

His message was received with a grunt as Mr Ross-Pitt bent over the operating table; the girl was in good hands now, so he forgot about her, absorbed in a tricky bit of surgery which demanded his powerful concentration.

At the end of the day Mr Ross-Pitt remembered Henrietta again, though. It would do no harm to make sure that Mrs Gregg was looking after her. He stopped the car outside a small flower shop near the hospital gates, picked a bunch of daffodils and narcissi at random and drove to Mrs Gregg's house.

Waiting for her to open the door, he felt impatient; he had had a long day and he would have to spend the night at his flat. It was imperative that he visited his patient later that night and if necessary in the early morning; the quiet evening that he had been looking forward to would have to be curtailed.

The door opened at last and Mrs Gregg stood aside and allowed him to enter.

'Upstairs I was, sir; came as quick as I could. Do you want to see Henrietta?'

'Please. I understand her doctor has been?'

'S'right. In a bit of an 'urry, but took a look at 'er. Told 'er ter take them pills regular and come and see 'im if she wasn't well in a few days.'

They had been climbing the stairs as she spoke; now she opened the attic door and stood aside to let him into the room. 'Ere's yer doctor, love.' She went on, 'And while yer 'ere I'll see to them cats.'

Henrietta sat up in bed, aware that she wasn't looking her best. Her hair felt like damp seaweed, she was hot and sticky, and she was wearing a grey cardigan over her nightie. She said, 'Hello,' in a gruff voice and eyed him with peevishness. 'I'm much better...'

'I am glad to hear that. I was passing and hoped you wouldn't mind me calling to enquire.' He laid the flowers on the bed and she put out a gentle finger to touch them.

'For me? How very kind. They're beautiful. Thank you, and thank you for calling. I really am feeling better. I shall get up tomorrow.'

'You will stay in bed tomorrow,' he told her quietly, 'and on the following day, if you feel well enough, you may get up. You will take things easily for the rest of the week. Presumably your doctor will sign you off as fit for work when he thinks it right.'

'Well, yes, I'm sure he will. I must write to Mrs Carter…'

'I'll leave a message with Reception.'

'Oh, will you? How kind.' She smiled at him from a white face, and he thought uneasily that she should be in more comfortable surroundings.

'Have you lived here long?' he asked.

'A few years.' She didn't enlarge on that, and he didn't ask any more questions for he guessed that she wasn't going to tell him anything. Presently he wished her goodnight and went away, escorted by Mrs Gregg.

'I'll look after 'er,' she assured him. 'Independent, that's what she is. Never a word about where she came from nor nothing about 'er family. Always ready to give an 'and—'elps that greengrocer on 'is stall of a Saturday afternoon. Well, every little 'elps, don't it?'

'Which reminds me,' said Mr Ross-Pitt, putting a hand into his pocket.

Two days later Henrietta got up, assuring Mrs Gregg that she felt fine and that there was no need for that lady to toil up and down the stairs any longer. 'There's plenty for me to eat in the cupboard. I must owe you a lot of money…'

'That doctor wot brought you 'ere, he asked Mr Biggs

where 'e could get milk and such and, Biggs being a greengrocer, 'e fetched what was wanted.'

'So I owe Mr Biggs?'

'Well, that doctor paid for everything.'

'Oh, dear, I'll have to write him a note and ask him how much I owe him. Mrs Gregg, I don't suppose there was a message from the offices?'

'Yes, there was. One of the girls wot brought you 'ere sent a note ter say yer job's still waiting for yer.' Mrs Gregg eyed her anxiously. 'But you'll not be going back until the doctor says so.'

'Of course not,' said Henrietta, not meaning a word of it. 'Thank you for looking after Dickens and Ollie.'

Monday was only two days away. Over the weekend Henrietta swallowed her pills, ate the contents of her cupboard, shutting her mind to what they had cost and how she was ever going to pay for them, washed her hair and made her plans.

She didn't think she had better go back to the hospital on Monday. She hadn't been to the doctor, and she supposed that she would have to wait for him to tell her that she might go back to work. No one knew about the offices, though—only Mrs Gregg, and she didn't get up very early. Henrietta reckoned that she would be back in her room by the time her landlady was up and about.

She had to admit to herself that she didn't feel as well as she had hoped as she caught the early bus on Monday morning. Probably the weather, she told herself; bitter cold and an icy wind. 'Going to snow,' said the conductor, taking her fare.

The other cleaning ladies were glad to see her back. 'Cor, we was afraid you'd get the sack,' she was told. 'Lucky you came this morning; there's plenty wanting to step into yer shoes. OK, are yer?'

Henrietta agreed that she was perfectly OK, donned her apron and got to work. It was the prospect of losing her job which kept her on her feet. The vacuum cleaner was like lead, the bucket of soapy water she needed to clean the paintwork weighed ten times as much as it usually did, and when she polished the desks they danced drunkenly under her eyes.

She managed to finish on time, however, put away her cleaning equipment, assured everyone that she felt fine, and, wrapped in her elderly coat, left the building to catch the bus.

Mr Ross-Pitt, driving himself home after an urgent summons to the clinic to do what was possible for Mr Wilkins, who had been found moribund in the street by one of the volunteer helpers, saw Henrietta walking with exaggerated care along the icy pavement. He stopped the car and got out and faced her, and since her head was bent against the wind she didn't see him.

'You little fool,' he observed, in a voice so cold that her head shot up to meet his eyes, which were as cold as his voice. 'Have you no sense? Are you doing your best to get pneumonia?'

He took her arm and bundled her into the car. 'You will go back to your room and go back to bed and try for a little common sense.'

He started the car and drove in silence, and Henrietta sat without saying a word; she felt peculiar for one thing, and for another she really couldn't be bothered to think of anything suitable to say. Besides, Mr Ross-Pitt was angry—coldly and quietly furious with her. She closed her eyes and dozed off.

He turned to look at her as he stopped before the house. She was asleep, long lashes curling onto her pale cheeks, her mouth slightly open. In no way was it possible to consider her pretty, even passably good-looking, and yet he found himself smiling a little, wishing that she would open her eyes. Certainly she couldn't go back to that attic room.

He got out of the car and knocked on the house door. Mrs Gregg, dressed but with her hair still in curlers and a pink net, opened it.

'Well, would yer believe it? What's up, Doctor?'

'I have brought Miss Cowper back to her room. I cannot think why she should be out in the streets at this hour.'

'Lor' bless yer, sir. Coming 'ome from her cleaning job. Goes every morning, though she didn't say nothing ter me about going terday.' She peered past him to the car. 'In the car, is she? Well, she won't be going to the 'ospital this morning, that's a cert.'

'Indeed not. Would you be so good as to pack a few necessities for her? She should be in hospital for a day or so until she is quite recovered. Obviously she isn't capable of looking after herself.'

Something in his voice warned Mrs Gregg to keep quiet about that. 'I'll pop upstairs and bring a bag out to the car,' she promised. 'Wot about them cats?'

Mr Ross-Pitt sighed. 'The cats... I'll return within the hour and collect them; my housekeeper will look after them until Miss Cowper returns here.'

'Suits me. I got enough ter do without being bothered with cats.'

He went back to the car and found Henrietta still asleep. She was a nasty colour, and every now and then she gave a little rasping cough. He picked up the car phone and dialled the hospital. He had had an almost sleepless night and a heavy day's work ahead of him; now he had saddled himself with this foolish girl and her cats. He glanced at his watch and asked to speak to the medical officer on duty.

Mrs Gregg came presently and handed over a cheap cardboard case. 'You'll be back?' She sounded anxious. 'I'll 'ave ter know if she's going ter be away long—'er rent's due—and then there's the cats.'

He put the case in the boot. 'I'll be back, Mrs Gregg, and we can settle things then. Expect me in an hour.'

He drove to the casualty entrance of St Alkelda's and watched as Henrietta was wheeled away, awake now but not at all sure of where she was. Indeed, she felt too ill to bother.

'I suspect pneumonia,' observed Mr Ross-Pitt to the young medical houseman on duty. 'Good of you to admit her. Entirely her own fault; she had flu and went back to work at some unearthly hour this morning. I'll speak to Dr Taylor presently.'

He got back into his car, leaving the houseman agog with curiosity. Mr Ross-Pitt was liked and respected; he expected his students to work hard and his standards were high, but he had never been known to rebuke any of them before anyone else and he was fair. He was always ready to listen to the young surgeons in his team and he was a splendid lecturer. On the other hand no one knew anything about him.

The houseman, making his way to the women's medical wards, decided that he would say nothing. Probably some employee—a domestic working for him, wherever he lived.

He wasn't so sure about that when he examined Henrietta. She was awake now, feverish and fretful, but she answered his questions in a small, husky voice and thanked him politely when he had finished. A pretty voice, he decided, despite the huskiness, and an educated one.

He wrote up his notes ready for Dr Taylor, went to see the ward sister and took himself off to breakfast, uneasy at Henrietta's anxious enquiry as to Dickens and Ollie, whoever they were. He had told her easily that they would be taken care of, but the memory of her anxiety stayed with him.

Mr Ross-Pitt, back at Mrs Gregg's house, wasted no time. He suggested once more, in a voice which compelled her to agree, that he should take the cats with him. 'My housekeeper will look after them until Miss Cowper is well again,' he repeated. 'Is there any rent owing?'

That was more like it. She said at once that there would be two weeks to pay on Wednesday. He was aware that this wasn't true, for she didn't look at him as she said so, but she probably needed the money. He paid her and fetched the cats, with Dickens indignant at having a cloth tied over his box while the kitten cowered beside him.

'I'll be in touch,' said Mr Ross-Pitt, and drove himself to his flat. He deposited Dickens and Ollie by the fire, offered refreshment and went to bath and change, wasting no time over it as he was due to operate later that morning. Over breakfast, cooked by the cleaning lady who came each day, he applied his powerful brain to his problems.

Henrietta was, for the moment, dealt with. There remained the cat and kitten, sitting by his fire, watching him anxiously. There also remained Henrietta's future. It was unthinkable that she should go back to that attic room, where she would probably get ill again unless there was someone on hand to make her see sense. Another job was the answer, of course—somewhere where she could have the cats and work reasonable hours. That would settle the question nicely.

He gave careful instructions to the cleaning lady about

Dickens and Ollie and then left for the hospital. There was no time to do more than go straight to Theatre, where he became at once immersed in his list—a lengthy one—starting with a craniotomy to arrest haemorrhage from a meningeal artery and ending hours later with a delicate operation on an elderly man with Parkinson's disease.

He was in Sister's office, having a cup of coffee and a sandwich before he went to the outpatient's clinic at three o'clock, when Dr Taylor phoned him.

'I've examined this girl you brought in, Adam. Pneumonia. I'll keep her in on antibiotics—they should do the trick. A bit under the weather, though; she could do with a week or two off work, whatever she does.'

'She works part-time in Occupational Therapy, and I believe she has an early-morning job, cleaning offices.'

'Really? She doesn't seem the type. No family?'

'I believe not. If someone comes to visit her, perhaps Sister could find out?'

'Yes. I'll keep you posted.'

'Thanks, Bob. Next time I'm at Occupational Therapy I'll see if Mrs Carter can't give her a full-time job. There's always the chance that she has friends or family who will help her.'

He put the phone down; Henrietta was all right for the moment; he had done what he could for her. But surely there were friends...? He went off to his clinic.

It was after six o'clock by the time he had seen his last patient, and he thought with relief of his drive home, with Mrs Patch waiting with a delicious meal. First, though, he had to go and see Henrietta.

She was awake, her face flushed, her hair plaited severely, a hospital nightie several sizes too large hardly adding to her appearance. Mr Ross-Pitt accompanied Sister to her bed and stood looking down at her.

'I'm glad to see you looking more comfortable,' he told her kindly. 'I hope you will do exactly as Sister says so that you may get well as quickly as possible.'

She stared up at him. He made it sound as though she had been a naughty small girl, but how could she expect him to understand? He lived in a different world, where there was always money in his pocket and abundant food and drink in the larder. She said, 'Dickens and Ollie...'

'Ah, yes, I have them safe. If you agree I will let my housekeeper look after them until you are well again.'

'You're kind. Thank you. She won't mind?'

'Not in the least. When you are discharged I'll arrange for them to be brought back to you.' He sounded brisk and impersonal. 'Goodbye, Miss Cowper.'

She closed her eyes as he walked away. She wasn't going to see him again, after all; he had been kind, especially taking Dickens and Ollie to his home, but she had sensed his impatience. Of course, he didn't want to be saddled with her; he had been angry and she thought that he still was. She must hurry up and get well and get back to work again...

It was a good thing that she didn't know that her cleaning job had already been given to someone else, and Mrs Carter, when apprised of her illness, had immediately gone to see the hospital manager and demanded that she had a replacement at once.

'She's bound to be off sick for some time,' she pointed out, 'and I simply must have more staff.' She added mendaciously, 'Her family will want her to go back home; she can probably get a job out of London.'

Mr Ross-Pitt drove to his flat, spent ten minutes with his secretary in his consulting rooms on the floor below, and

then fed Dickens and Ollie, put them back in the cardboard box and took them down to the car, making a
mental note to purchase a suitable cat-basket. Not that
either of them gave him any trouble. They had had a
bewildering day and huddled together on the back seat,
making no sound.

He drove fast, anticipating a quiet evening with no
need to return to his consulting rooms until the following
early afternoon. He would have to call in to the hospital
to check on his patients, but even so he wouldn't need
to leave home until noon. It was with quiet pleasure that
he saw the lighted windows of his house, and a moment
later Mrs Patch opened the door, allowing Watson to
dash past her to greet his master.

Mr Ross-Pitt stopped to fondle him. 'Hello, old fellow. I've a surprise for you.' He picked up the box and
bore it indoors. 'Mrs Patch, you have no idea how pleasant it is to be home—and I have brought a problem with
me.'

The box he was holding heaved, and Mrs Patch said,
'Lawks, sir, an animal—?'

'Two. A cat and a very small kitten. I will tell you
about them presently. Could they stay in the kitchen for
the moment? If I put their box by the Aga, perhaps they
could have a saucer of food? They've had a tiresome
day.'

He went along to the kitchen, leaving a puzzled
Watson in the hall, and undid the cloth over the box to
meet Dickens' baleful eye. Mrs Patch, without asking
questions, found a saucer, chopped up cold chicken from
the fridge and set it close to the box. A saucer of milk
was put down too, and then Dickens and Ollie were left
to themselves.

Over a glass of sherry Mr Ross-Pitt explained. 'There
was really nothing else to be done,' he observed, topping

up his housekeeper's glass. 'I hope that it will be for a short time only. I suppose I could find a cattery...'

'No need, sir. Once Watson's seen them and they're a bit used to us they'll be no trouble. I'll be sure and keep them indoors to start with. And the young lady? What about her? Poor child.'

'Well, it's really no concern of mine, Mrs Patch, but unfortunately she appears to have no family, and her living conditions are appalling. Perhaps I should ask around and see if there is more suitable work for her.'

'Young, is she?' asked Mrs Patch. 'A young lady?'

'Both young and ladylike, if that isn't too old-fashioned a word to use.'

Mrs Patch tut-tutted, then asked, 'Pretty?'

'No. No, not in the least. The cat and kitten are our immediate problem; you are sure you can manage?'

'Lord bless you, sir, of course I can. Watson and I will look after them.'

Rather to his astonishment there were no difficulties. Dickens, introduced cautiously to Watson—thoroughly upset since his little world had come adrift—accepted the dog's friendly approach, and the kitten, too small to know better, wound himself round Watson's legs. If his friend Dickens accepted Watson, then he would too.

The next afternoon Mr Ross-Pitt drove himself back to London; Henrietta and her cats could be shelved for the moment. He enquired as to her condition when he got to the hospital, was reassured that she was responding to treatment, and promptly forgot about her. It wasn't until he was on the point of driving home that he remembered to leave a message for her to say that Dickens and Ollie were safe and well.

They had settled down nicely, Mrs Patch told him

when he got home that evening, and Watson had adopted them without fuss.

'Splendid,' said Mr Ross-Pitt, and spent an agreeable evening catching up with his reading, Watson draped over his feet, a wary Dickens sitting before the log fire, and Ollie bunched up beside him.

'I only need a wife sitting on the other side of the hearth,' mused Mr Ross-Pitt, 'to be completely domesticated.'

It was two days later that he chanced to meet Dr Taylor in the consultant's room. 'That patient of yours, Adam—she's doing very well. Up and trotting round the ward. Fit to go home in another three or four days. Asked her if she had family or friends to go to; she was a bit vague—said she would be quite all right, had somewhere to go. Nice little thing.'

That afternoon Mr Ross-Pitt found time to go to Occupational Therapy. Mrs Carter came to meet him. 'You've come to see Miss Jenkins? She's doing splendidly.'

He spent some time with that lady, expressed his pleasure at her progress, and as he went away asked, 'Mrs Carter, is there a chance that Miss Cowper could be employed full-time? She has been ill, as I'm sure you know—'

Mrs Carter laughed. 'They say it's an ill wind... I wouldn't wish the girl harm, but from my point of view things couldn't have turned out better. I saw the hospital manager as soon as I heard about it, and I have a full-time replacement. Henrietta will get a week's notice when she leaves hospital—paid up, of course.'

She glanced up at him, smiling with satisfaction, and took a step back. He wasn't frowning—there was no expression on his face—but she knew that he was very

angry. All he said was, 'Ah, yes, quite so, Mrs Carter.
Good day to you.' He had gone before she could say
another word.

He contained his rage with an iron hand and went to
see the medical ward sister. Henrietta was doing well,
she told him; did he wish to see her? 'No, there is no
need, but will you let me know when she is to be discharged?' He smiled suddenly. 'My housekeeper has
charge of her cats.'

Sister smiled too. 'I'll leave a message at Reception,
sir. And she's been a good patient.'

There was something else which he had to do. That
evening he went to see Mrs Gregg, who opened the door
to him looking so guilty that he knew what she was
going to say.

'Let 'er room sir; couldn't 'elp meself, now could I?
Need the cash, and not knowing when she'd be back.
'Er bits and pieces are in a case, and the furniture's in
the basement. Got somewhere to go, 'as she?'

'No, Mrs Gregg, she hasn't,' he said gently, 'but I
don't suppose that will worry you unduly.' He turned to
go and she called after him.

'Wot about 'er furniture? It can't stay here...'

'Dispose of it, Mrs Gregg.'

He was glad of the drive home; it gave him time to
think. Whether he liked it or not, it seemed that he was
saddled with Henrietta and her cats. A job and a home
for them must be found within the next few days, and
there was no likelihood of either.

Beyond a ward round and a handful of private patients
in the morning, Mr Ross-Pitt had little to do the following day. He drove back directly after lunch to spend an
afternoon walking Watson and catching up on his post.

In the evening he had been bidden to dine with the

owners of the big mansion which dominated the other end of the village. He knew them well, for they had lived there all their lives, inheriting it from ancestors and managing somehow to preserve it for their children by opening the house and grounds to the public on several days of the week.

Their youngest daughter had just become engaged, and the dinner was to be a black-tie affair in her honour. When he arrived there he found the sweep in front of the house already full of parked cars.

He was too old a friend to stand on ceremony, greeting their elderly butler with a gentle slap on his shoulder and going straight to the drawing room.

Lady Hensen put up her cheek for his kiss. 'Adam, how nice to see you—Peter's at the other end of the room with Felicity and Tony. I suppose you're up to your eyes in work; we don't see enough of you. It's time you found a wife; I'm longing to dance at your wedding.' She laughed up at him, still a pretty woman, with kind eyes and a serene manner.

He found Sir Peter, congratulated Felicity and her fiancé, and then wandered around greeting other friends. He was well-known and popular, and Lady Hensen had seen to it that he was seated between two of the prettiest girls there. They were intelligent and amusing as well as pretty, and he enjoyed his dinner.

It was some time later that he found himself with Lady Hensen. She patted the sofa beside her. 'Sit down for a while, Adam; here is a chance to talk, for probably we shan't see you again for weeks. Tell me what you've been doing with yourself, other than bending over the operating table.'

'Very little, I'm afraid. I quite often need to stay in town overnight, and it's difficult to arrange anything in case I'm wanted. When I'm here there is the garden to see to and Watson to take for walks.' He smiled. 'I think I must be solitary by nature.'

'Only until you find the right girl. Did you know that we are planning to open on five days of the week instead of four? We did quite well last year and hope to do even better. Of course, the difficulty is finding people to work for us. Not everyone is keen to be buried in the country...'

'What kind of people?' he asked idly.

'A girl Friday! Isn't that what they are called? Someone who will turn her hand to anything, and I mean just that. The young just don't want to know; they want bright lights and discos and money to buy clothes, and the wages we offer are paltry.'

Mr Ross-Pitt turned a suddenly thoughtful face to her. 'She would live in and get her food and so on?'

'Well, of course. She'd have to share one of the lodges, but we certainly feed our employees...'

'In that case, Lady Hensen, I believe I know of just the right person.'

CHAPTER THREE

LADY HENSEN gazed at him. 'You mean you actually know of someone who might like a job? A girl?'

'Let me explain...' Which he did, giving her the facts in an impersonal voice. 'She is normally a healthy girl, surprisingly tough. Used to hard work and looking after people.'

He hesitated. 'I suppose she is that old-fashioned thing—a lady fallen on bad times, I imagine. There is one problem; she has a cat and kitten.' He smiled suddenly. 'I've got them at present—there was nowhere else for them to go. She is to be discharged from hospital in a few days' time and has nowhere to go.'

'The poor child. I'll speak to Peter, and if he agrees she can come here and see how she gets on. A week's notice on either side and she's welcome to bring the cat and kitten. She can have a room in the south lodge with Mrs Pettifer. She will have to work hard—make her understand that.' She paused. 'Not physical hard work so much as being at everyone's beck and call...in a nice kind of way.'

'You are very kind; I'm sure she will be delighted to have work and a roof over her head. Also away from London.'

'She doesn't like town?'

'Not that part of town where she is living at present— or rather was living. You would wish to see her before you employ her?'

'No. No, Adam—you vouch for the girl; that's good

44

enough for us. As I said, let her come and see how she gets on. Will she be fit to start work in a week's time?'

'As far as I know, yes.'

'Then I'll speak to Peter this evening. Shall she find her own way here?'

'I'll bring her.'

He went back home with the pleasant feeling that everything had been nicely settled. He would have to find out when Henrietta was to be discharged. If that was to be before the week was out he would have to arrange for her to stay somewhere. Tiresome, he thought with impatience, but the last of the obstacles before she could be settled and hopefully become a vague memory.

He told Mrs Patch his plans the next day. 'We shall have to keep Dickens and Ollie for another few days. I'll bring Miss Cowper with me once everything is arranged, and we can collect them on the way to Lady Hensen's.'

'When will that be, sir?'

'Oh, within the week, I hope. If she is discharged before then I'll get my secretary to find her lodgings for a couple of days.'

Which was exactly what happened.

Four days later, Henrietta, warned that she was to be discharged on the following day, was swallowing sudden panic when Sister said, 'You're to go to the manager's office; he'll explain things.'

She was a busy woman, so Henrietta didn't waste time asking questions but presented herself before a bad-tempered-looking girl who looked up from her computer long enough to say, 'Through that door.'

The man on the other side of the door looked just as bad-tempered. 'Miss Cowper? You're leaving us, I'm told. Here's your back pay, and you can apply for a reference if you should need one.'

'Leaving?' Henrietta drew a breath and willed her voice to remain steady. 'It's the first I've heard of it.'

He looked uncomfortable. 'Lack of communication somewhere. The chief told me that Mrs Carter had said you had family who wanted you home again. I sup- pose no one told you since you weren't well... Is there some- where...? You're going home now?'

She gave him a steady look. 'Yes, I'm going home now.' She even smiled. 'Good afternoon.'

She went back to the ward and found Sister. 'Will it be all right if I go home now?' she wanted to know. 'It would be much more convenient for my family if I went today. I'll get a taxi...'

Sister looked doubtful. 'We did say tomorrow. On the other hand I do need your bed. You'll be all right? There will be someone there when you get home?'

Henrietta thought of Mrs Gregg—she was someone, wasn't she? So she wasn't fibbing, just being a bit mis- leading, perhaps, but Sister wanted her bed anyway. 'Yes, there'll be someone there. I'll be in nice time for tea.'

Sister, picturing a happy family reunion round the tea- table, gave her permission. Henrietta didn't waste time; she said hurried goodbyes to her fellow patients, thanked the sister and took herself off. She had two weeks' pay in her purse, but she wasn't going to squander any of it on a taxi. She joined the queue and stood at the bus stop.

Mr Ross-Pitt, a satisfactory afternoon's work behind him, remembered that Henrietta was to be discharged on the following day. He would have to go and see her and arrange to pick her up and take her to the respectable boarding-house that his secretary had found for him. In two days' time he would collect her once again—hopefully for the last time, he reflected—and take her to Lady Hensen's.

He should have gone to see her and explained that there was a job waiting for her, that Mrs Gregg had let her room and that she had got the sack from Mrs Carter, he thought, but he had had busy days and busy nights, and it would be easier to explain to her in person, rather than sending a message or a note.

Sister was in her office writing the report.

'May I see Miss Cowper for a few moments? I've not had a minute to talk to her.'

'Henrietta? But she's already gone, sir. Discharged not an hour ago. She went to collect her pay, I suppose. Said she'd take a taxi and there would be someone waiting for her at home.'

He preserved an admirable calm. 'A pity. Never mind; it's my fault for not making the time to come sooner.'

'It was all right—letting her go? I have warned the office. Actually, it was providential, for I need her bed desperately.'

'Quite all right, Sister.' He bade her a courteous good evening and went away without apparent haste.

She would have gone to Mrs Gregg's, he reflected as he got into his car. He only hoped that she was still there.

She was—standing on the doorstep, listening to Mrs Gregg's voice, which was loud and belligerent because she felt guilty. He cut into her diatribe without apology. 'Henrietta, thank heaven you're still here. I never meant this to happen...'

She turned to look at him. 'What did you mean to happen?' she asked. Her voice was as stony as her look. 'Someone could have told me.'

'Let me explain.'

'There is no need. Besides, how does one explain how I have come to get the sack without being told, to have my—my home rented to someone else the moment I turn my back, and to lose my furniture and my cats?'

She had spoken quietly, but he could see that she was on the verge of tears. Mrs Gregg raised her voice once more and he withered her with a look, took Henrietta by the arm and popped her into the car before she could protest.

'How dare you?' said Henrietta. 'Stop the car at once; I wish to get out.'

'Not here, you won't. You'll sit there while I explain.'

'And apologise. I hope you realise that—that...' She faltered to a halt.

'Yes, of course. I realise everything.' He heard a watery sniff. 'Have a good cry while I tell you what has happened. I make no excuses; I've been busy, but somehow I should have found the time to come and see you. I'm sorry. There's a great deal I have to say; I suggest we go somewhere and have a meal while I explain.' He gave her a quick, sidelong glance. 'I don't know about you, but I'm famished.'

Henrietta blew her nose. 'So am I, but I have to find somewhere—'

'That's arranged. I'll tell you about it, only don't keep interrupting.'

He started the car, leaving Mrs Gregg still talking although there was no one there to hear her. 'My case,' said Henrietta.

'I'll collect it tomorrow; we can find things for you for the night.'

She opened her mouth to speak at that, but closed it again. He had said that he would explain.

He drove a short distance and presently stopped in a busy shopping street, parked the car by a meter and opened her door. 'I'm short of time, but we can get a meal here while I talk.'

The café-restaurant was small and only half-full. He asked her what she would like, and when she hesitated offered to order for her. When the waitress had gone he observed, 'I'll be as brief as possible; save your questions until I have finished, will you?'

He guessed what she wanted to hear first. 'Dickens and Ollie are with my housekeeper, happy and safe. No, don't say anything. I tried to get Mrs Carter to take you on full-time but I was unsuccessful. I didn't know that no one had told you that they had given you the sack. Believe me, if I had known that I would have let you know somehow. I went to see Mrs Gregg and found that she had already let your room and put your furniture in her basement.'

He paused while a large pot of tea was put before her. It looked heaven sent, but she didn't take her eyes off his face.

'If you would consider it, there is a job waiting for you. Friends of mine who live south of Thaxted—know it?—need someone to work for them. A girl Friday is, I believe the correct term. Their house is in the country and it is open to the public five days a week. I presume you will be a jack of all trades, but they are very kind people and the country around is delightful.

'You may have your cats with you, but you will share one of the lodges with someone called Mrs Pettifer. The pay is small, but you'll be fed and housed.'

Henrietta poured their tea and someone put a plate loaded with bacon and egg, baked beans and crisp fried bread before her.

'Well,' said Henrietta, and took a sip of tea. 'I thought I didn't like you at all, that you said things you hadn't meant just to be rid of me, but it's not like that at all. I have been thinking awful things about you, and all the time you've been kind and helpful and there was no need—you don't even know me... I'm very grateful.'

He said impatiently, 'Never mind all that. Eat your supper; I can spare rather less than an hour. My secretary has found somewhere you can spend the next two days. For heaven's sake, though, don't go tearing around on some senseless idea or other. I will fetch you in two days' time, in the evening, so be ready to come with me. You're going on a week's trial, but I see no reason why you shouldn't stay there for as long as it suits you. Have you any decent clothes?'

Henrietta loaded her fork daintily with baked beans and popped them into her mouth. When it was empty she spoke.

'I know you don't mean to be rude,' she told him kindly, 'but if you talk to your patients like that I'm surprised that you have any! No, I have no decent clothes. I am wearing my best now. Everything else is in my case at Mrs Gregg's.'

He was glad to see that she had recovered her spirit, but he didn't say so. 'You had better go shopping for essentials tomorrow. How much money have you?'

'Wait while I count it,' she begged him, and did so. 'Forty-five and forty-five is ninety, and there's four pounds sixty pence and a few coppers in my purse. That's ninety-four pounds and sixty pence—two weeks' wages, and what was left over from the week before.' She added sharply, 'What happened to my jamjar? There was a week's wages from the office block in it, and my savings...'

'How much were you paid for this cleaning job?'

'Twenty-five pounds a week. I'll have to go back to Mrs Gregg and ask her about it. I—I can't afford to lose it.'

Mr Ross-Pitt concealed his feelings admirably. 'No,

no, of course not. I'll get it when I go for your case tomorrow. Eat your supper, Henrietta, and listen to me. I think you could afford to spend around seventy pounds on clothes. The rest you can save for that rainy day and, since there's nothing to spend your money on where you are going, you will be able to add to it.

'I will get the money from Mrs Gregg, and supposing I suggest that she sells the furniture? You won't need it, at least for the time being, and if nothing is done about it she will dispose of it without telling you.'

'Will she? But I might want it again.'

He suppressed a shudder. 'I doubt if it will stand up to being stored in a basement. Be brave, Henrietta; burn your boats.'

She smiled then—she had a lovely smile, lighting up her whole face. 'Yes, all right, I will. You're sure that it is all right to spend all that money?'

Mr Ross-Pitt, who spent twice that amount on taking any one of the women of his acquaintance out to dinner, assured her that it was.

She offered him more tea, and although he didn't want it he passed his cup because he guessed that she wanted another cup herself. It was a powerful brew, richly brown, loaded with tannin. He swallowed it with apparent pleasure and presently suggested that they should go.

The house he took her to was near the hospital, on a corner of a street which, while having seen better days, was by no means as shabby as those surrounding it. Its owner, Miss Lodge, was elderly, austere and determined to keep the standards by which she had lived in her youth.

She accepted only hand-picked lodgers, insisted on being paid on time, and that there should be no what she called 'hanky-panky', but she fed them well, kept their rooms spotless, and hidden beneath her high-necked blouse was a heart of gold.

She received Henrietta briskly, shook Mr Ross-Pitt's hand, told him equally briskly that there was no need for him to wait and then stood aside while he bade Henrietta goodnight. 'You will remember all that I've told you,' he reminded her. 'I shall be unable to see you before I come to fetch you, so be sure and get everything that you are likely to need.'

'Dickens and Ollie? Will you bring them with you?'

'They're at my home—I live near Lady Hensen, your future employer. We'll collect them on our way.'

She offered a hand in its shabby glove. 'You are very kind, and thank you for my supper.'

He looked down at her. Her eyes were beautiful, he decided. 'A pleasure,' he told her in the kind of impersonal voice she wasn't sure that she liked. It made her feel as though she were his patient. Which was exactly what he had hoped.

Miss Lodge led the way upstairs. 'Your room is small, but as you are here for such a short time I thought it would be sufficient for you. The bathroom is on the same floor. Kindly do not spend more than twenty minutes when using it; there are six other boarders on this floor. I gather that you have had a meal, but if you wish for a cup of tea you are welcome to come to the kitchen and make yourself one.

'Breakfast is at eight o'clock—several of my boarders have an early meal, necessary so that they may get to their work on time. I don't provide lunch or afternoon tea, but there is high tea at six o'clock. You are welcome to sit in the sitting room during the day.'

Henrietta said thank you and added that she would have to do some shopping and would probably be away for most of the day. Miss Lodge nodded graciously. 'So

I understand. Doubtless you will need to fit yourself out for your new job.' And at Henrietta's enquiring look she added, 'I was informed of your circumstances, Miss Cowper.'

She had opened a door to disclose a small room, rather crowded with furniture, but it was clean and cheerful and the bed looked comfortable.

'I'll leave you to come down for tea if you wish. You will find everything you need for a night or two in the top drawer of the dressing table.'

'Thank you, Miss Lodge; how very kind and thoughtful of you.'

'I have done what has been requested of me,' said Miss Lodge austerely, and went away.

Henrietta waited a few minutes before opening the door and going in search of the bathroom—a chilly apartment which made no attempt to attract, but where the water seemed hot and the bath was spotless. She thought it unlikely that anyone would dare to leave it otherwise than pristine.

There was no one in the kitchen when she found her way there, but there was a teapot and a tin of teabags on the table, and mugs and a milk jug. She made her tea and then went back upstairs, intent on a bath.

The drawer had yielded a plain cotton nightie, a brush and comb, soap, towel and face flannel. At least she would be clean, and in the morning she would get face cream and powder and a lipstick. She would have to make a list... First, though, she would bath.

The water *was* hot; she could have stayed for a long time, going slowly lobster-pink, her mind nicely blank, but Miss Lodge's stern words about the period allowed in the bathroom sent her back to her bed with minutes to spare.

She was sleepy now, but the list had to be made. Quite

short, for there wasn't much money. She whittled it down to the absolute necessities before she at last curled up and slept.

Miss Lodge presided at the breakfast table in the morning, keeping a stern eye on her lodgers. There were four of them present besides Henrietta—two young women and two older men. None of them spoke much—polite good mornings, then requests to pass the butter or marmalade, and an equally polite 'excuse me' as they left the table.

Henrietta ate her porridge, the boiled egg by her plate and a slice of bread and butter, drank the tea that Miss Lodge poured for her and, since there was no one left by then, offered to help clear the table.

Miss Lodge looked surprised. 'No, thank you.' She sounded friendly. 'I think that you should go and do your shopping. Ring the doorbell twice when you return. You may make yourself some tea if you wish when you come in.'

Henrietta thanked her. She felt delightfully full with her wholesome breakfast; it was amazing what a good meal did for one. The future looked hopeful, and the thought of seeing Dickens and Ollie again cheered her.

She put on her coat, tied a scarf over her hair, since she had no hat, and took herself off to spend her seventy pounds. It would have been nice to spend it in the big stores in Oxford Street, but there such a small sum would have melted away like snow. Instead she found her way to the local market, where there were stalls of jackets and anoraks, woollies and cheap skirts.

She didn't hurry over her choice but priced everything carefully before first buying a pair of sensible lace-up shoes—not leather, of course, but they looked as though they were. That seen to, she turned her attention once more to suitable clothes for her new job.

The skirt she was wearing was one of Oxfam's best, but it had seen better days; she found a grey and black checked skirt, teamed it with a grey sweater and one patterned with several shades of blue and green, and then went in search of a charity shop.

She found a quilted jacket there, so cheap that she was able to spend the last few pounds on sensible undies and two nighties, totally lacking in glamour but promising warmth; winter was by no means over yet.

She had coffee and a sandwich after that, pleased with her purchases and lingering over her small meal in the overheated little café. And then, since she had no more money to spend, she made her way back to Miss Lodge's house, where she was admitted, told to wipe her feet before she crossed the hall and told to make herself a pot of tea if she wanted it. 'And there's bread and butter if you're hungry,' said Miss Lodge severely.

The tea was good, hot and strong, and a slice of bread and butter was welcome. These disposed of, Henrietta went to her room and examined her shopping, stifling a wish that she could have bought delicate silk undies and fashionable clothes if only she had had the money. What she had bought, she told herself stoutly, was exactly right for the job she was going to, and once she had settled in there and she felt sure of staying she would save up and gradually collect the sort of clothes she longed for.

She tried everything on, craning her neck to see as much as possible of herself in the small looking-glass. Really, the jacket fitted very well; no one would know that it had come from Oxfam...

Mr Ross-Pitt, coming to fetch her the following day, recognised the coat unerringly as a garment from a charity shop, but he was a kind man. He told her that she looked very nice, had a short session with Miss Lodge, and then took Henrietta and her case and went out to the car.

It was dark and chilly and the car was delightfully warm, smelling faintly of good leather. He got in beside her, observing, 'I saw Mrs Gregg—she offered to buy your furniture for twenty pounds, and I accepted on your behalf. I hope I did right?' When she nodded he added, 'She hopes that you will be very happy. I have your jar in the boot—she counted it with me. Thirty-one pounds, sixty-four pence.'

Henrietta did some sums in her head. 'So I've got more than seventy-six pounds.' She sounded quite breathless with relief.

'Indeed you have,' he agreed gravely, 'and you will be paid at the end of each week. Have you all that you need? We can stop if you want to buy anything else.'

'No—I think I've enough of everything to start with, thank you.'

'Then shall we go?'

'Yes, please. I hope I'm not spoiling your evening.'

'Not at all. I'm going home, and it is no trouble to drop you and the cats off.' He heard her satisfied sigh and hoped that he would be forgiven for the fib about Mrs Gregg's offer to buy the furniture.

'I've thrown it out,' she declared when he'd asked her about it. 'A load of old rubbish—got the men ter cart it away.'

If he hadn't been insistent, she would have denied having the jampot… Henrietta need never know that he had added the twenty pounds from his own pocket—a trifling sum, but it was obvious from his quick, all-seeing glance that she needed every penny she could get.

He set himself to put her at her ease as he drove, and she answered his mild observations politely, but he could sense that she was nervous. He began to tell her something of the Hensens' home, describing it and the people who lived there, telling her amusing stories of the visitors who came to look around. 'I dare say that when you've got used to things you will be asked to act as guide sometimes. You like old buildings?'

'Yes, I do, although I don't know much about them. Churches and museums, of course, but you see I've never met anyone who owned a large house.'

'They are rather a responsibility; the upkeep is never-ending.'

He had left the main road by now and was driving along a narrow country lane, and presently the village came in sight. He drove along its main street, through his gates and stopped at his front door. Henrietta peered out.

'Is this it? It looks lovely—like something out of a fairy story.'

He had opened her door, and helped her out. 'This is my home; come in and collect Dickens and Ollie.'

'You live here?'

'With Mrs Patch, my housekeeper, and Watson.'

Watson came tearing through the open door to greet them.

She bent to stroke him. 'He's lovely—I've never had a dog... Does he mind Dickens and Ollie?'

He led her indoors. 'He's been a father to them. Come and see them; they'll be in the kitchen.' He paused to greet Mrs Patch, who had come into the hall.

'Henrietta, this is Mrs Patch, who looks after me wonderfully well. Mrs Patch, this is Henrietta Cowper, come to collect her cats.'

Henrietta offered a hand, and Mrs Patch shook it

firmly and smiled. 'I'll miss them and no mistake; they've not given me a moment's trouble.'

'I am glad; it's so very kind of you to have looked after them, Mrs Patch.'

'There's coffee waiting, sir,' said Mrs Patch. 'I'll bring it to the drawing room right away.'

'Excellent. Henrietta, let me take your jacket.' Which gave him a chance to see the skirt and the more sober of the woollies. Adept at concealing his thoughts, he didn't allow her to see what he thought of her appearance; his face remained friendly and faintly aloof and she felt reassured; he was, she decided, a man who didn't notice things like clothes.

Relieved by this mistaken assumption, she sat down in one of the easy chairs as Mrs Patch came back with a tray and, trotting behind her, Dickens and Ollie.

'Good as gold,' said Mrs Patch smugly, 'and they know you're here, miss.'

Henrietta had got out of her chair and was on her knees, Ollie tucked under one arm while she stroked Dickens. 'Oh, they look so fat and well.' She looked up at Mr Ross-Pitt, politely standing. 'I can never thank you and Mrs Patch enough; you've been so kind.'

'Think nothing of it. It is Mrs Patch who has had far more to do with them than I. Come and sit down and drink your coffee.' He watched his housekeeper pour, and went on casually, 'We found two cat-baskets, but I dare say one is sufficient, for Ollie is still very small. I think it may be best if we leave them in the car while you meet Lady Hensen, and then I will take you down to the lodge where you are to live.'

'Yes. Yes, of course, Mr Ross-Pitt,' Henrietta decided that he was impatient to see the last of her, and no wonder. She drank her coffee, refused a sandwich from the

plate that Mrs Patch offered and declared herself ready
to go.

No time was wasted. The basket was fetched and
Dickens and Ollie settled into it with a bit of old blanket
while Henrietta reiterated her thanks to Mrs Patch, trying
not to look at the sandwiches. She was hungry; they had
left Miss Lodge's house before high tea, and lunch had
been a sketchy affair, but to keep Mr Ross-Pitt waiting
was unthinkable after all he had done for her.

He settled her and the cats in the car, aware of relief
at the thought that she would now be settled and he
could forget her and get on with his life.

It was surprising how large she had loomed during the
last few days. He supposed that that was because he felt
responsible for her. That was ridiculous, he reflected as
he drove back through the village and in through the
Hensen's park gates. She was a young woman who had
obviously become used to fending for herself; probably
she would have been perfectly all right if he hadn't in-
terfered…

He stopped the car outside the imposing entrance and
got out to open her door. 'The south lodge is about five
minutes' walk from here; I'll drive you there, presently.
Come along.'

He hadn't meant to sound brusque, but she hurried
beside him, all at once a bundle of nerves. How awful
if, after all his trouble, she should prove unsuitable.

The butler who admitted them looked kind; he bade
Mr Ross-Pitt good evening, smiled at her and said, 'Lady
Hensen will see you straight away, miss. If you will
come with me.' He glanced at Mr Ross-Pitt. 'If you
would like to wait in the morning room, sir, there's a
fire there.'

Mr Ross-Pitt put a hand on Henrietta's shoulder. 'It's
better if you're on your own. I'll wait.'

He watched her lift her chin and put back her shoulders as she followed the butler across the hall.

She hadn't known what to expect. The relief at the sight of Lady Hensen's kind face was so great that she felt quite dizzy.

'Come here, Miss Cowper, and sit down. We'll have a little talk and then Adam can take you down to the lodge. He has spoken so highly of you that I feel I know quite a lot about you already. I'm sorry you've been ill— you do feel up to working?' Henrietta nodded.

'To start with, I'm afraid, you will be doing all the odd jobs no one else has time for, but later, when you know the place and have settled down, I think you might be suitable as a guide. They're all part-time, fitting in whenever and wherever they can, so you will be most useful.

'You will have Sunday mornings free until one o'clock, and every Tuesday for the whole day. I should want you to start work at eight o'clock each morning, after breakfast at the lodge with Mrs Pettifer, then a short break for coffee mid-morning, your midday dinner at twelve o'clock and supper at half past six. Sometimes these times are altered—if we are away, or have guests or some special event.

'Did Adam tell you what your wages would be? Fifty pounds a week and your board and lodging—not very highly paid for a fifty-three hour week, but we will look after you and treat you fairly.'

'I'm very grateful to be given the opportunity to work for you, Lady Hensen, and I'm quite content with the wages and the hours. Thank you for letting me have Dickens and Ollie here too.'

The door opened then, and Sir Peter came in and Henrietta got to her feet. He was a short, stout man in early middle age, with a round, merry face and twinkling eyes. 'I've just been talking to Adam. So this is Miss Cowper—what's your name, my dear?'

'Henrietta.'

'That's better. Coming to work with us, are you? We can do with an extra pair of hands. My wife will tell you everything you need to know.' He went to the door. 'I'll see you around tomorrow morning, I dare say.'

He had gone, and his wife said, 'Sir Peter is devoted to this house; it has been in his family for a very long time. Now, I won't keep you any longer; you'll want your supper and bed.' She pulled the bell rope by the fireplace. 'Feathers, take Henrietta back to Mr Ross-Pitt, please, and ask him to come and see us on his way home.'

Henrietta said goodnight and followed the butler back to the hall, where she was told to wait while Mr Ross-Pitt was fetched.

'Everything all right?' he wanted to know, and hardly waited for her answer. 'Let's get you down to the south lodge…'

The lodge was at the bottom of a second drive—a small picturesque cottage beside the big wrought-iron gates—and its small door was opened as he stopped the car, got out, helped Henrietta out and collected the cat-basket.

Urged forward by his hand between her shoulders, Henrietta paused in the doorway. Mrs Pettifer was there, and so unlike her imagining that she was dumb. She had expected a country woman, small and stout, possibly in an apron and possibly resentful of having to share her home, but Mrs Pettifer was none of these things.

She was tall and thin, with sharp features, spectacles on a high-bridged nose and an immaculate hair-do. She was well dressed, too, but her voice when she spoke was pleasant and welcoming.

'Henrietta Cowper, how very nice to have company. Come along in, and you too, Mr Ross-Pitt. You have the cats with you? Good. You'll be wanting your supper and bed?' She led the way from the minute lobby into the sitting room, small and rather crowded with furniture, but there was a bright fire burning and the lampshades were very pretty.

'Time for a drink?' Mrs Pettifer asked Mr Ross-Pitt, and when he said that he was going back to the house she nodded. 'Of course. We won't keep you.'

'I'll get Henrietta's case.' He put it down in the lobby and turned to her. 'I'm sure you're going to be very happy here; I expect I shall hear great things of you.'

She offered a hand and said quietly, 'I shall do my best, and thank you again for your help. Goodbye, Mr Ross-Pitt.'

He took her hand in his large, firm grasp and she wished that he would never let it go—a wild thought that she instantly dismissed. He said goodbye to Mrs Pettifer then, and drove away. It was like losing a slice of her life, thought Henrietta.

Mrs Pettifer cast her a sharp glance. 'Come and see your room,' she suggested. 'You can take off your coat and then we'll have supper and I'll give you some idea of your day's work. Shall we let the cats out in the kitchen? I got a few tins of cat food, but I see Mr Ross-Pitt has left some too. Through here...'

The kitchen was small but nicely equipped, with a table and two chairs up against one wall and a dresser built into a recess by the stove. The stove was warm, and when Henrietta undid the basket Dickens and Ollie crept towards it.

'I'll leave their saucers here—and I've provided for their needs...' Mrs Pettifer waved towards a large tray just inside the open door of what looked like a lean-to.

'The bathroom's here.' She opened another door and showed a miniscule room. 'And my room is opposite the sitting room. The other bedroom is upstairs. It is small but I hope you will like it. You'll share the place with me—treat it as your home. I really am glad to have company; it can be lonely here in the evenings.'

Henrietta followed her up the narrow stairs to a room built into the roof. It had dormer windows and sloping walls, but the wallpaper was pretty and the narrow bed against one wall was covered by a thick quilt. There was a chest of drawers with a mirror on it, a small chair and a bedside table and a row of hooks along one wall.

'It's lovely,' said Henrietta. After her attic it was a small, cosy heaven.

Mrs Pettifer looked pleased. 'Good. Come down and eat your supper; you must be famished.'

Supper was a casserole, with baked apples and cream for afters. Henrietta ate everything put before her, helped with the washing-up and then sat opposite Mrs Pettifer in the sitting room, Dickens and Ollie crowded onto her lap, while that lady outlined her duties. 'Plenty for you to get on with,' she observed drily. 'I don't suppose you can sew?'

'Well, yes—not dressmaking, but mending and darning and hemming sheets.'

'Hemming sheets! Good Lord, Henrietta, you sound like someone from a Victorian orphanage.'

'Well, I am,' said Henrietta. 'I mean I was sent to a children's home when I was six and I stayed there until I was twenty-one. That's years longer than is really allowed, but I taught the little ones...'

'Well,' said Mrs Pettifer. 'I can see that Mrs Dale, who's in charge of the repairs—curtains and covers and so on—will welcome you with open arms. Now, go to bed, my dear. Have you a clock? No? Then I'll give you a call at half past six.'

So Henrietta bade her goodnight, settled Dickens and Ollie in a cardboard box in the kitchen and went up the narrow stairs, to creep down again presently to have a bath. Mrs Pettifer, still sitting by the fire, didn't appear to see her, though her sharp eyes had seen Henrietta's coat over her nightie.

If anyone needed the job, she reflected, Henrietta did. Even if it were only to allow herself to get a dressing gown.

CHAPTER FOUR

REFLECTING on her first day as she settled into bed the following evening, Henrietta decided sleepily that she had enjoyed every hard-working minute of it. Fortified by Mrs Pettifer's sensible breakfast of porridge, boiled egg and toast, washed down with strong tea, she had accompanied her to the house.

Ushered in through the side-door, she had been introduced to the domestic staff—the cook, the butler, the housekeeper, two housemaids, the kitchen maid and someone called Mrs Croke, in a sacking pinny and wearing a felt hat, who came each day from the village, and had told her that she 'did' for Lady Hensen.

Henrietta had shaken them all by the hand and, told by Mrs Pettifer to go with Addy, one of the maids, had gone. They had dusted and vacuumed the dining room and she had found time to look around her as she worked. It was a magnificent room, panelled with some dark wood, furnished with an enormous sideboard and a vast dining table.

From there they had gone to the drawing room, where she had vacuumed while Addy cleaned the grate and laid a fire. Then they went upstairs to make beds and tidy bedrooms while Sir Peter and his lady breakfasted, and by the time they had finished and returned to the kitchen their coffee was ready. There had been thick slices of bread and butter too...

After that the cook had sent her out to the head gardener down at the greenhouse to fetch rhubarb. 'There's plenty of jackets by the back door,' Cook had said. 'Be sure and take one, and a pair of boots…'

The head gardener was a crusty old man, with whiskers and hands crooked with arthritis, but he had been kind to her, and when she had admired the clumps of violets tucked away in one corner of the greenhouse he had told her gruffly that they would be brought to the house and potted in time for Lady Hensen's birthday. 'Fancies a nice violet,' he had added. 'Like 'em do you?'

'Oh, yes.' She had turned a happy face to him. 'You see, I've never really seen flowers growing—only bunches on market stalls.'

She had hurried back with the rhubarb and been told to take a tin of beeswax and a pile of dusters to Mrs Pettifer. 'In the ballroom,' the butler had said. 'Go into the hall and down the passage to the right of the dining room.'

Mrs Pettifer had been on a stepladder, dismantling a pair of ormolu wall-lights. 'Put them down, Henrietta; thank you. Come here and take these as I hand them to you.'

Henrietta had stayed with her until they'd been bidden to their midday dinner—stewed beef and dumplings and a jam roly-poly pudding for afters…

Henrietta, now half-asleep, came awake again at the mere delicious memory.

She had been kept busy for the rest of the day, and when she'd got back to the lodge she and Mrs Pettifer had tidied up the little place, lighted the fire, fed Dickens and Ollie and had a pot of tea between them. When she had gone upstairs to bed Mrs Pettifer had told her that if she liked to keep her door open she might have Dickens and Ollie with her. 'We can try and see what happens. Of course, if they disturb us in the night then they will have to stay in the kitchen.'

Henrietta put out a hand in the dark and felt their furry bodies pressed against her, and was instantly asleep.

After the first day the next few went rapidly. She had been given, as it were, a taste of everything—helping the cook, polishing the furniture, hanging out the washing, running to and fro saving Mrs Dale the housekeeper's legs. She hadn't seen either Sir Peter or Lady Hensen; the butler and one of the maids waited at table, carried in trays and answered the front door.

Once or twice she had thought about Mr Ross-Pitt. It would have been nice to see him again, but since that was unlikely she didn't waste time on that except to reiterate in her mind her gratitude towards him.

She still couldn't quite believe that she had such a splendid job, that she was saving money—or would be soon—and that Dickens and Ollie were happy and safe. They had quickly made themselves unobtrusively at home and even, after that first day, ventured into the tiny patch of garden behind the lodge, thereby earning Mrs Pettifer's approval.

Of course, she didn't know what to do with her free day. She got up as usual and had breakfast with Mrs Pettifer, who told her that she could go to the house for her dinner if she wanted to. 'Or go into Thaxted,' she suggested. 'It's a nice little place, with some quite good shops.'

She didn't say any more, for she had seen the look on Henrietta's face. Of course, the girl probably had no money to spend. 'Why not go for a walk and get your bearings?' she suggested kindly, and that was what Henrietta did.

The village was small, cosily arranged around the church, with a prosperous-looking pub opposite and a war memorial on the green. There was a village shop and post office and, by taking a roundabout way, she was able to get a good look at Mr Ross-Pitt's house.

It was larger than she had thought, and when she went down a narrow lane leading away from the main street she found that it led to the fields beyond, from where she had a splendid view of the back of the house. It rambled without rhyme or reason under its tiled roof, small windows in its gables, its walled garden bounded by a little stream.

She stood and looked at it for a long time, imagining him coming home to its peacefulness each evening, taking Watson for a walk, eating the meals his housekeeper cooked for him. 'A bachelor,' she mused out loud. 'I suppose he's so wrapped up in his work that he hasn't found the time to marry.'

She wandered on, happy to be free, but feeling hungry. She could, she supposed, go to the pub in the village, but she felt shy at going there alone.

It was a stroke of luck that presently she reached a second lane which led to a cluster of cottages, one of which had a sign hanging above its door with 'Teas' written on it. It was early for tea, but perhaps at this time of year that wouldn't matter. A pot of tea and a bun, thought Henrietta, fingering the money in her purse.

She was warmly welcomed; customers were few and far between so early in the year. She had her pot of tea and a plate of buttered toast and the owner lingered to talk.

'New around here, aren't you?' she asked in a friendly way. 'We don't see many strangers at this time of year. Staying roundabouts, are you?'

Henrietta explained that she was working for Sir Peter Hensen. 'I've only just started, but I like the job very much.'

'They're well liked,' agreed her companion. 'The

family's been there since I don't know when.' She chuckled. 'Well, you might say half the village is lived in by folks whose ancestors were here hundreds of years ago. Look at that Mr Ross-Pitt—his family have been living in that house of his for I don't know how long. Know him, do you?' She didn't wait for Henrietta to answer. 'You won't have had time to meet him yet, and he's away in London most days. By way of being highly thought of, so I've heard.'

When Henrietta got up to go she was told to come again whenever she wanted to. 'Tibbs is the name. My old man works for the builders over at Thaxted and the boy's working on a farm in Shropshire. It's a bit lonely in the winter.'

'I'd like to come again,' said Henrietta. 'Not next week, though, for I must go into Thaxted and buy one or two things, but I'll come again soon! Can I bring you anything when I come? I don't know what the shops are like there...'

'Good enough for me—there's a supermarket and any number of small shops. There's nothing I need, but you never know—thanks for the offer.'

Henrietta went back to the lodge then, and set the table for their supper, fed Dickens and Ollie and accompanied them into the garden for a while. It was chilly still and she went indoors to light the sitting-room fire, presently to sit by it with Dickens and Ollie lying in her lap. She sat there daydreaming, until a glance at the clock reminded her that Mrs Pettifer would be back soon and it was time to get some supper.

'Enjoyed your day?' asked Mrs Pettifer as they sat down to scrambled eggs and mushrooms and a pot of tea.

Henrietta told her where she had been, and said that yes, she had had a lovely day.

'Mrs Tibbs is a very good sort—does well with her teas in summer, but she must be a bit lonely there at this time of year. There are mostly old folk in the other cottages.

'Lady Hensen wants me to start on repairing the curtains in the big hall; I'll want you to come along and give me a hand. It's close work, so we can do only a few hours at a time, but the tourists don't come in any numbers until Easter.'

'I'll do my best,' said Henrietta. It would be a pleasant change from being at everyone's beck and call. Not that she minded that—everyone had been very kind and helpful, even the housekeeper, who was probably not as severe as she looked.

The curtains were very old, and almost threadbare where the heavy striped silk was stitched to the lining. Henrietta perched on a carved oak armchair of great age, spread the curtain on the Pembroke table before her and set to work.

Mrs Pettifer, coming in presently, said nothing and started on another curtain, but later, when it was time for them to go to the kitchen for their mid-morning coffee, she came over and inspected Henrietta's work.

She took off her spectacles and looked at Henrietta. 'A rare thing, to find a girl who can sew. Lady Hensen will be pleased.'

Henrietta, long used to Mrs Carter's depressing comments about her work, glowed with content.

She was finding her feet by now, not only around the house but among its occupants. Mrs Pettifer was hardly a domestic; she was head guide during the tourist season, she was in charge of the rooms open to the public, and she was entrusted with the cleaning and the care of the silver and porcelain on display.

The housekeeper ruled the staff with a firm hand—with the exception of the butler, Feathers, whom she consulted on any knotty problem which might arise. The housemaids were friendly and so were the two gardeners and the odd job man, who came up from the village each morning. In the season, Mrs Pettifer had told her, several ladies in the village helped with the guide work and helped in the small tearoom in the grounds.

Henrietta was told to go to the housekeeper's room on Friday morning and was given her weeks' wages. She went back to her sewing, her head filled with delighted thoughts. No rent to pay, no bus fares, no food to buy—on her next day off she would go to Thaxted and spend a little of the money in her pocket. The rest she would put away; there was always the chance that Lady Hensen would decide that she wouldn't do and she must add to her tiny capital so that she had some security against being out of work again.

She had still seen nothing of Sir Peter or Lady Hensen, and although Mrs Pettifer was kind and friendly she hadn't passed many opinions on Henrietta's work.

'I didn't tell you, did I?' said Mrs Pettifer that evening. 'You are free on Sunday morning—' Henrietta nodded. 'You know that. I'm free from one o'clock. Do what you like in the morning—I'll have breakfast as usual, but you get yours when you like. Church is at eleven o'clock if you would like to go, and midday dinner is at half-past twelve on Sundays. It's quiet at this time of year and there are no guests this weekend.

'You'll be needed to sit in the office leading from the entrance hall, to answer the phone and listen for bells. Everyone else will be off duty until about half past three, when one of the maids will get the tea if anyone is home.

You'll have your tea as usual, and stay in the office until six o'clock.

'Supper is in the servants' hall on Sundays—half past six. You're free after that. I think you might take some work to do while you're in the office. That torn cushion cover from the great hall…'

Henrietta said, 'Yes, Mrs Pettifer,' and added, 'Might I be allowed to come here to feed Dickens and Ollie? They usually have something directly after midday dinner.'

'I don't see why not, as long as you tell someone where you are and don't stay too long.'

So when Sunday morning came she didn't get up until Mrs Pettifer had left the lodge, when she went downstairs and, with the cats for company, had a splendid breakfast before tidying up, making her bed and getting ready to go to church. She had no hat, which bothered her a bit, but she looked tidy if nothing else. Besides, there was no one to see her and she would sit at the back of the church.

It was a ten-minute walk, and the bell ceased to ring as she reached the porch. The church was quite full but she slipped into a pew by the door, said her prayers and then looked around her.

Almost under the pulpit was an enclosed pew with a little wooden gate and a coat of arms on it. Sir Peter and Lady Hensen were sitting there—she could see Lady Hensen's hat and Sir Peter's grey head—and on the other side of the aisle was Mr Ross-Pitt. Her heart gave a lurch at the sight of him and then dropped to her shoes at the sight of the lovely, elegant young woman sitting beside him.

Although why I should be surprised I don't know, reflected Henrietta. Of course they'll be going to marry... Her thoughts were brought to an end by the entry of the choir and vicar, and by dint of singing hymns very loudly and listening to every word the vicar said she was able to dismiss Mr Ross-Pitt completely from her head.

She'd intended to slip out of the church before the rest of the congregation, but she hadn't reckoned on the fact that everyone waited until the Hensens had led the way. Mr Ross-Pitt, waiting his turn like everyone else, saw Henrietta and made shift to follow the Hensens' progress, taking his companion with him, so that by the time they had left the church he was close behind them and in time to prevent Henrietta sliding away before he spoke to her.

She looked better already, he reflected while deploring her drab clothes. There was a healthy pink in her cheeks, however, and her uncertain smile made her almost pretty.

'Henrietta—how nice to see you. How are you?' He smiled, his voice as kind as his words. 'You look splendid...' He turned to his companion.

'Deirdre, this is Henrietta Cowper, who works for Sir Peter. Henrietta, this is Miss Stone.'

Miss Stone looked Henrietta over. 'Oh, really? One of the servants?'

'Yes,' said Henrietta before Mr Ross-Pitt could speak. 'How do you do?' She spoke frostily, and then turned to Mr Ross-Pitt.

'I'm very happy—you have no idea—' She stopped; he wouldn't want to know more than that. 'I have to go back for my dinner. It was nice to see you again.' She added 'sir' in a defiant little voice, which made him wince. She smiled at them both, and slipped past them and out of the churchyard.

Deirdre said languidly, 'Really Adam, what odd people you know.'

He said placidly, 'There is nothing odd about Henrietta.' He glanced at his watch. 'We will go back home and I'll get the car out—we're due to go for drinks with Lady Hensen.'

Deirdre took his arm. 'Darling, what a bore, and I suppose Mother will want to come as well...'

'Why not? She has been invited.'

Mrs Stone was sitting by the fire, a wisp of a woman, dominated by her daughter. She looked up as they went in; Deirdre looked petulant, and she sighed.

She hadn't wanted to visit Adam; she was aware that Deirdre was determined to marry him and she was also aware that he had no intention of doing so, but, since she and his mother were old friends and it had been suggested that she and Deirdre should break their journey on their way north, she had reluctantly agreed to spend a night on their way. A waste of time, she considered; Adam had been a perfect host, but if he felt anything more than casual friendship for Deirdre he was concealing it very skilfully.

He would be, of course, a splendid catch, and Deirdre had so far failed to find herself a husband, but Mrs Stone knew better than to point that fact out to her daughter. Life was sometimes difficult living with her; Mrs Stone promised herself that one day she would speak her mind to Deirdre, but so far the worm hadn't quite gathered enough courage to turn...

Henrietta, relieved to have escaped from Miss Stone's malicious eyes, walked back to the lodge, attended to Dickens and Ollie, and went up to the house for her dinner. The food was good and ample; she was tucking into Cook's treacle pudding when the housekeeper, who had her meals in her own room, came into the servants' hall.

Agnes—one of the maids—had tripped on the back stairs and hurt her ankle, she informed them, and Lady Hensen had asked any number of people back for drinks. Feathers couldn't manage by himself, and Addy the second maid was off duty.

'Henrietta, go along to the drawing room and make yourself useful.'

Henrietta swallowed a mouthful of pudding and got to her feet. No one argued with the housekeeper.

There were a dozen people standing around the drawing room. No one I've met before, reflected Henrietta thankfully, bidden to carry a tray of sherry to a group at the other end of the room. Too late she perceived that she had been mistaken; Mr Ross-Pitt was there, and Miss Stone.

She offered the drinks, and when she proffered the tray to the pair of them, who were standing a little apart from the others, she kept her eyes on Miss Stone's expensive leather belt, and then on his waistcoat buttons.

'Hello again,' said Mr Ross-Pitt easily.

She ignored that; it didn't seem right to offer drinks and say hello to guests at the same time, not when she was doing her best to look like Agnes.

'Oh, it's that domestic we saw in church,' said Deirdre languidly. 'Well, I suppose it makes a change to see how the other half live.' She laughed, and Henrietta's hand tightened on the glass she was offering.

Inured to rudeness though she was, having to leave her half-eaten pudding and serve drinks without being given a moment in which to powder her nose or tidy her hair and, on top of that, meeting Mr Ross-Pitt again was too much for her normally level-headed nature.

'No, no, Henrietta, don't,' said Mr Ross-Pitt softly,
and she uncurled her fingers and offered Miss Stone the
tray of drinks. That lady had been looking at him, expecting him to share in her amusement, and she was
gratified to see the smile lurking at the corners of his
mouth. Only his smile wasn't for Deirdre.

Henrietta slid away back to Feathers. He sent her to
get a napkin for the vicar's wife, who had spilt her sherry
on her dress, and while she was mopping her up Lady
Hensen crossed the room. She commiserated politely
over the stain, recommended remedies and turned to
smile at Henrietta.

'What a treasure you are, Henrietta.' She looked at
the vicar's wife. 'Adam Ross-Pitt recommended her to
me, and I shall never cease to thank him.' She raised her
voice to say 'Adam,' so that he turned round enquir-
ingly.

'Come here and say hello to Henrietta; you will be
pleased to know that she is everything you said of her.'

He came unhurriedly. 'We met in church this morning…'

Henrietta had had enough. 'Excuse me, Lady Hensen,
but Feathers is beckoning me…' Her vague, polite smile
embraced all three of them.

She never wanted to see him again, she told herself
fiercely as she trotted to and fro under Feathers' eagle
eye, horribly conscious of her unsuitable clothes. She
wasn't likely to get the chance either. The guests went
presently and he with them, without so much as a glance
in her direction.

Sitting in the office later on with the big house quiet
around her, Henrietta had time to think. Clothes, she
decided. Not for the world would she risk again having
to appear at a moment's notice in the clothes she had

bought so hopefully in London. They would do well enough for her daily chores, but there had to be one decent garment that she could get into, and shoes other than the useful lace-ups she wore.

Recklessly she decided to spend the whole of her fifty pounds on her day off. Her mind made up, she turned her attention to the cushion cover. Inevitably her thoughts returned to Mr Ross-Pitt.

The jangling of a distant bell disturbed her. She knew which one it was—the old-fashioned contraption which hung beside the little door at the side of the house. It opened from the garden onto a passage which led to the main hall and was used by the family and servants and no one else.

Henrietta went to answer it; one of the staff had gone for a walk, she supposed, and forgotten to take the key kept hanging in the passage. She took it from its hook now and pulled back the bolts as the bell rang again.

She unlocked the door with a breathless, 'Sorry you had to wait,' and found a young man—a stranger—standing there.

He smiled at her in a friendly fashion. 'This place is like a tomb on Sunday afternoons out of season. You're new, aren't you?'

He made to come into the house, but Henrietta stood solidly in his path.

'Yes, I'm new. Would you tell me who you are? Did you want to see someone?'

'You're as fierce as Mrs Pettifer; she terrifies me, but somehow I don't think you're fierce at all. I'm Mike Hensen—Sir Peter's my uncle. Now may I come in? He'll be in his study having a nap, so you can come with me and make sure that I'm not intent on carrying off the family silver!'

She stood aside then. He seemed genuine—well-dressed, pleasant voice and manner, good-looking too. She wasn't sure if she liked him, but that wasn't to say that he wasn't a perfectly nice person with nothing to hide.

It had been pleasant to be spoken to as his equal, she reflected as she led the way to Sir Peter's study. She paused outside the door. 'Sir Peter doesn't like to be disturbed—' she began.

He grinned at her. 'Scared to knock?' he asked.

Henrietta said, 'Certainly not,' and thumped on the door rather harder than she had meant to. Sir Peter's voice, coming thickly through its solid panels, sounded impatient. She opened the door then and stood aside to let the visitor in. 'Mr Mike Hensen to see you, sir,' she said, giving what she hoped was a good imitation of Feathers' manner.

Sir Peter got up. 'Come in, Mike—this is a pleasant surprise.' His eye fell on Henrietta. 'Thank you; bring tea in half an hour will you, Henrietta?'

The kitchen was deserted. She laid a tray, and wondered about cake and sandwiches, and felt relief when Cook appeared.

'Sandwiches,' she said crossly. 'And that means there'll be two teas to get, for Lady Hensen won't have hers a minute before half past four. Drat the man.' Cook began opening cake tins. 'Run along to the office, my girl, I'll see to this. Come back in half an hour to carry the tray.'

Young Mr Hensen was lolling in a chair when she went back with her laden tray. He made no move to help her, and the thought that Mr Ross-Pitt would have got to his big feet and taken the tray from her flashed through her mind. She must stop thinking about him, she told herself, speeding back to the kitchen, where Cook had poured her a cup of tea.

'Take it with you, and there's a plate of sandwiches.'

Henrietta thanked her and went back to the office once more. The tea was hot and strong, and Cook had been generous with the sandwiches. She ate the lot, carried the tray back, washed her hands and went back to her mending—an occupation conducive to thought.

Because she didn't want to think about Mr Ross-Pitt she thought about young Mr Hensen instead. It wasn't fair to judge someone by first impressions, she told herself; he had been friendly, not like that awful Miss Stone.

She wondered if Mrs Patch liked her, and what about the dog, Watson? Deirdre didn't look the sort of person to enjoy a dog's company.

I'm being mean, Henrietta decided. I don't know a thing about her; she might be perfectly charming. But I don't like her.

That evening, when supper was over and she and Mrs Pettifer were sitting comfortably by the fire in their little sitting room, that lady told her a little about young Mr Hensen.

'A nephew,' she explained. 'His parents live in the States but he chooses to live in England—he's got some kind of job to do with computers and suchlike. Sir Peter has a son at Cambridge, but I think Mike hopes for some part of the estate when Sir Peter dies. He has several very profitable farms. Mike comes here a good deal; it's his second home.'

She stroked Ollie, lying in her lap. 'Did you get the cushion cover mended?'

Henrietta took the hint; she was to be told nothing more about the Hensens. 'Very nearly; I was hindered for a while.'

'Yes, of course, I was forgetting. You managed very well.'

Henrietta went pink. Praise, even in its mildest form, was delightful to hear. She ventured, 'I came on a week's trial, Mrs Pettifer...'

'So you did. Since you've heard nothing I think you may take it that you're here on a permanent footing.' Mrs Pettifer glanced across at her. 'What are you going to do with your day off?'

'Go to Thaxted and do some shopping. There are quite a few things I need.'

Her companion nodded. Henrietta's wardrobe was scanty to say the least.

'There are one or two quite good outfitters—not expensive, but plenty of choice. I have bought several things there—a jersey skirt and cardigan are both useful with different blouses. I should not be telling you this, but I believe that Lady Hensen is considering you as one of our guides once the tourist season starts—you have plenty of time to get a nice little wardrobe together before then.'

A piece of news which, upon reflection, caused Henrietta to add some of her savings to the fifty pounds. It made sense to get one or two suitable outfits. Even if by some evil chance she lost her job at least she would have a better chance of getting another if she looked decently dressed.

There was an early morning bus to Thaxted from the village. On Tuesday Henrietta joined the queue, the quilted jacket buttoned over the second sweater, a scarf over her hair, her handbag with its precious contents tucked under one arm. She had the day before her, and she couldn't wait to start her shopping.

She was deep in thought, weighing the advantages of tweed against blue serge, when Mr Ross-Pitt drew up beside her. He opened the car door and said briskly, 'Get in, Henrietta.'

She was the last one in the queue, and the two men ahead of her were deep in talk. 'I'm going to Thaxted,' she told him, and then added, 'Good morning, Mr Ross-Pitt.'

'Let us be civil by all means. Get in, Henrietta.' When she shook her head he said, 'I'm going to Thaxted; I'll drop you off.'

Something in his voice caused her to get in, followed by one of the men's voices. 'That's right, ducks, do as you're told; you'll come to no harm.'

'Well, really,' said Henrietta crossly. She wanted to add to this rather useless remark but didn't know how. Instead she said frostily, 'This is very kind of you, Mr Ross-Pitt.'

'Considering that I'm already late and you have wasted several precious minutes, yes, I am kind. Is this your day off?'

'Yes. I'm sorry if I've made you late, but you need not have stopped.' She added reasonably, 'I could have caught the bus—'

'For God's sake, stop harping on the bus, Henrietta.'

After a couple of minutes of heavy silence he said, 'All right, I know I'm in a bad temper; take no notice.'

'Well, I wasn't going to,' she told him kindly. 'We all have our bad days.'

'You more than most.'

'Well, yes, perhaps, but not any more. I'm very happy now, and I'll never be able to thank you enough—' His irritable grunt stopped her. It was strange, but seeing him so testy made her feel uneasy. Something must have upset him badly...

Presently he asked her, 'What are you going to do with your day? Shopping?'

'Yes, I do need quite a lot of things.' They were on the outskirts of Thaxted and he slowed the car, not speaking again until he drew up in the main street.

'Don't get out,' said Henrietta. 'You're late—you said so. Thank you for the lift, Mr Ross-Pitt.'

He closed the door, lifted a hand and drove away. A bit rude, reflected Henrietta; not like him; he must be sickening for something.

Mr Ross-Pitt, racing towards London, would have been amused at that; he never sickened for anything. He had behaved badly, he mused; Henrietta hadn't deserved his ill-humoured remarks. He was, had she but known it, suffering from a surfeit of Deirdre's company.

Henrietta made for the shops, very certain about what she needed to buy. She wasn't going to be hurried; to spend so much money all at once was a serious matter and needed thought. She found the shop that Mrs Pettifer had recommended and bought a navy jersey jacket and skirt, mindful of that lady's words. She didn't think she looked her best in dark blue, and she was right, but she consoled herself by buying two blouses—one floral in muted pastel shades, and a navy and white striped one, with a neat little bow at the neck.

Pleased with her purchases, she went in search of shoes and was lucky enough to find a pair of plain black court shoes, half price in a closing-down sale, and that left enough money for a little velvet hat with a soft brim—navy blue again, but it was a useful colour.

There was very little money left now; she had a cup of coffee, bought stockings and some cheap gloves, and then spent the rest of the morning inspecting the shops, deciding what she would buy the following week. A raincoat, she decided—she hadn't enough money for a winter coat—and the week after that she would stock up with coloured sweaters, and the week after that... The list was never-ending…she wouldn't be able to save much for several months, but once she had some decent clothes she would save every penny.

By dint of eating an economical lunch, she had enough money to go to a chemist and purchase face cream and powder, shampoo and a lipstick. It was still early afternoon, so she went and sat in the church for a while before having a cup of tea in an Olde Worlde tea shop—all cretonne and with tables too large for one and too small for two—but the tea came in an elegant teapot, the china was pretty and the scones and butter were delicious.

She caught the bus back then and, since Mrs Pettifer wasn't at the lodge, set the table for their supper. She went into the garden with Dickens and Ollie, and then went upstairs, the cats with her, to inspect her purchases.

She showed them to Mrs Pettifer when she returned presently, and was pleased to see that she approved of them. 'I thought I'd buy something new each week,' she said.

Mrs Pettifer thought that that would be just as well; Henrietta was always as neat as a new pin, and she wore her shabby clothes with an air, but all the same she would be able to tell Lady Hensen that next time Henrietta was called upon to appear amongst her guests she would be suitably dressed.

'Not that I mind,' Lady Hensen had declared, 'but there are those who would make a joke of her, and I won't have that! You think she would do as a guide?' she had asked.

'Yes, I do. She'll need to learn about the place, of course, but she's quick and intelligent, even if she isn't much to look at.'

Lady Hensen had laughed. 'Mike thinks she's a *jolie*

laide with beautiful eyes. He's very taken with her. Not seriously, of course!'

Mrs Pettifer, discretion itself, had had nothing to say to this. Mr Mike was a nice enough young man, but careless and selfish and self-indulgent. It would amuse him to captivate Henrietta, who anyone could see knew very little about the world, and moreover would give her heart to anyone who wanted it. She had lacked love all the years of her life and was more than ready to offer it to anyone who showed the least inclination to need it.

She and Henrietta finished their supper, and as they washed up together Mrs Pettifer said carefully, 'Have you any idea that you might have some family somewhere?'

'I don't think so. I can remember Grandmother and Grandfather, but I don't think there was anyone else. Anyway, it's all so long ago that even if I had cousins or aunts and uncles I wouldn't know them, would I? And I'm sure they wouldn't want to know me.' She reiterated, 'I'm really very happy, Mrs Pettifer.'

Always, though, at the back of her mind, was the image of Mr Ross-Pitt's handsome face. Try as she would, she found it impossible to relegate him to a past best forgotten.

CHAPTER FIVE

WINTER was giving way reluctantly to spring. The sky, for so long uniformly grey, became for long periods a pale, washed-out blue and the sun shone with a tepid warmth. It rained a good deal, of course, but Henrietta, now the owner of a raincoat and a matching hat, didn't care.

Over the next couple of weeks she used her day off to good effect, adding to her wardrobe garments which would stand her in good stead for some time to come. She had been tempted once or twice to eschew these sensible clothes for something colourful and bearing the hallmarks of the latest fashion, but common sense warned her that, delightful though it was, a little pink wool jacket with its matching pleated skirt would look out of date in a year's time and she would have to wear it for a good deal longer than that.

She bought a beige jacket instead, long enough to pass for a winter coat and guaranteed to be unnoticeable for years to come. A pity Mr Ross-Pitt couldn't see her now, she thought wistfully as she tried it on, and dismissed the thought as useless. He might live in the same village but they never met. She saw him in church on Sundays, but only from the back, and she slipped away before the rest of the congregation had gathered up their gloves and hymn-books.

It was Mike Hensen who saw her from time to time; he was staying at the house, apparently on holiday. He had developed a habit of strolling around inspecting the public rooms which Mrs Pettifer, almost always aided by Henrietta, was getting ready for the expected flow of tourists around Easter.

There was a great deal to do—pictures to take down and dust and examine for repairs, great chandeliers to take to pieces, and each crystal drop to be carefully washed and dried and rehung, candelabra to be treated with the same delicacy, curtains to be taken down and examined for repairs and cleaning. Some of the ladies from the village came in to help, and Henrietta, for the first time in her life handling beautiful furniture and ornaments, loved every moment of the work.

She hardly noticed that Mike Hensen was often close by, watching her. Once or twice, when she had climbed a stepladder to reach a picture or ornament, she had found him steadying it for her, and she had thanked him politely and replied in her friendly way when he had made some joking remark, but she hadn't time to waste on idle chat; Mrs Pettifer, although kindness itself, expected her to work for her wages.

Mike was intrigued by her lack of interest in him. Women liked him—he was good-looking, well mannered and an amusing companion—but this rather drab girl was impervious to his charm. He was killing time before joining friends on a trip to India and he was getting bored; it might be amusing to coax the girl to fall in love with him... He would have to be discreet, of course, and that dragon Mrs Pettifer mustn't suspect.

It was pure chance that he happened to be in the village pub one Tuesday when Henrietta walked briskly by, making for the other end of the village. He finished his pint and then followed her in a leisurely fashion. He was surprised when she turned down the lane close to Mr Ross-Pitt's house, and waited until she was crossing the field beyond. There was nothing much beyond that, he knew—only a handful of cottages, and he could reach those by going the long way round and joining the lane half a mile away.

So it was that when he came upon her at Mrs Tibbs' door he was able to look surprised. 'Henrietta—are you enjoying a day off?' Then before she could answer him Mrs Tibbs came to the door.

'Come in,' she said at once, and then added, 'Mr Mike Hensen, isn't it? Out walking, are you?'

She looked from him to Henrietta with smiling curiosity.

'I don't know about Henrietta, but I've been hiking around for quite a time. I was hoping that you'd give me a cup of tea.'

Mrs Tibbs was charmed. A pity, he thought sourly, that it wasn't Henrietta, who merely looked faintly annoyed.

'Of course. Perhaps you'd share a pot? And I've baked some of those little cakes you liked last time, Henrietta, if you wouldn't mind?'

Henrietta had been looking forward to a half an hour's gentle gossip with Mrs Tibbs, but she hid her disappointment and said that no, she didn't mind in the least, and sat down at one of the little tables in Mrs Tibbs' crowded front room.

Mike sat down too, saying easily, 'This is kind of you—I don't think many people know about Mrs Tibbs...' He began to talk in a casually friendly way—the weather, the country around them, amusing little stories about the tourists—and never one question did he ask of her or probe her own life with.

He watched with satisfaction as she slowly lost her shyness and uncertainty about him, and when they had finished their tea it seemed quite natural for him to walk with her.

He said, 'If you care to, I can show you a rather nice

alternative route back to the other end of the village. It
makes a change—you came down the lane, I dare say?
This way takes a bit longer, but it's such a nice afternoon
that it seems a pity to hurry back.'

He talked of this and that as they walked, and
Henrietta found herself enjoying his company. Though
she had had very little to do with young men—the children's home had certainly not encouraged such friends—
and although she had got on well with those she'd met
at the hospital, none of them—the young men—had
shown any inclination to get to know her better. This
was something that she had accepted in her sensible way,
but Mr Hensen—she refused to call him Mike—had
made her realise how pleasant it was to spend time in
the company of a man of her own age—one who
laughed and joked and didn't ask questions.

They gained the village high street and paused outside
the village shop. 'Thank you for my tea,' said Henrietta.
'I enjoyed the walk too.' She smiled at him, and Mr
Ross-Pitt, driving himself home after a particularly trying outpatients clinic, saw the smile.

He drove past them with a casual wave and without
smiling. Henrietta, pink with the pleasure of seeing him,
swallowed her disappointment. She quite understood that
for him to stop and speak to her was unlikely, but he
could have smiled.

Mike Hensen, watching her face, smiled to himself
too. It would amuse him to turn her attention to himself
and away from Adam Ross-Pitt—a man he didn't like
overmuch; few people saw through Mike's apparent
charm and good nature—Adam was one of them. He
was sure that Adam had no interest in Henrietta other
than that of someone who had given her a helping hand,
but all the same...

Mike nodded goodbye and walked away, and

Henrietta went to the shop to buy toothpaste and soap and the chocolate mints that Mrs Pettifer liked.

It was on Sunday morning as she left the church that Henrietta came face to face with Mr Ross-Pitt. He had overtaken her easily enough as she crossed the church-yard to go out by the little wicket-gate at one side of it, and his hand on her arm pulled her up short.

He didn't bother with good morning. 'Avoiding me?' he asked.

And he smiled at her breathless, 'Good morning, Mr Ross-Pitt. No, of course not.'

He fell into step beside her. 'Good. Are you still quite happy working for Lady Hensen?'

'Yes. Oh, yes, thank you. It's... You have no idea...everyone is so kind...' As she spoke she realised that even if she had been unhappy she would never have told him; he had gone to a great deal of trouble to find her a job, and the least she could have done would have been to tell him how happy she was.

It was nice to be able to tell him the truth. She *was* happy; her days were long, and she had no time to her-self until the evening, but she had money in her purse now and new clothes. She was thankful that she was wearing the beige jacket and the velvet hat and her new shoes.

She asked him, 'Have you been busy at the hospital? You must be glad to have a quiet day here.'

'Indeed.' He smiled down at her. 'I'm almost always busy, but I must admit that I don't care for London. Coming back here at the end of the day is always a pleasure.'

She was anxious to be at her ease. 'How is Watson?'

'In splendid condition. Dickens and Ollie—are they nicely settled in?'

'Yes, Ollie has grown and Dickens has become quite handsome.' They had reached the gates to the manor and she paused. 'It is nice to see you again, Mr Ross-Pitt.' She held out a hand. 'I'm going back by the back drive; we don't use this front drive.'

'In that case I'll walk with you; I'm lunching with the Hensens and I'm early.'

She was aware of delight welling up her insides. They could never be friends, of course, but just to see him and speak to him made her feel happy and content. She longed to ask him about Miss Stone; the kitchen had it that he would marry her, but that had been gossip. All the same, she wished that she knew. If I knew, thought Henrietta, I would be able to stop thinking about him.

Mr Ross-Pitt was saying something. 'I dare say that you have discovered some of the walks around the village.'

She answered readily, 'Oh, yes. There's a cottage I go to sometimes on my day off—Mrs Tibbs; she has a tearoom by the lane on the other side of the fields beyond your house. Now I've found another way to it—at least, I met Mr Mike Hensen last time I went there and he showed me. He knows the country around here very well, he said.'

'A very pleasant companion,' agreed Mr Ross-Pitt mildly. 'It is nice that you have met someone of your own age.'

She was quite shocked. 'Oh, we're not friends. I mean, he's family, isn't he? I'm one of the domestic staff. We—don't mix.'

'What a good thing that I'm not one of the family,' observed Mr Ross-Pitt gravely.

She looked at him uncertainly, then decided that he was joking and smiled. 'Yes, isn't it.' And she added thoughtfully, 'Do you suppose it wouldn't do if I were to meet Mr Hensen—by accident, of course—and he stopped to speak to me?'

'I presume that Mike stops to speak to anyone in the village; there is no reason why he shouldn't pass the time of day with you, Henrietta.'

'But not go walking?'

'Perhaps not, but that is for you to decide. You see,' he added gently, 'the other staff at the house might resent it.'

'Yes, of course. Not that I particularly want to, you know, only it was rather nice to have someone to talk to. I wouldn't upset the others for the world; they're so kind. Cook gives me scraps for Dickens and Ollie, and the housekeeper lets me go to the ballroom to look at the family portraits...'

'Mrs Dale's bark is worse than her bite. You like Mrs Pettifer?'

'Oh, yes, very much. She knows everything.'

They had arrived at the lodge and she bade him goodbye and stood watching him walk away, watched in her turn by Mrs Pettifer from the sitting-room window.

'Don't look surprised,' she said as Henrietta went in. 'I came back to collect an address I had for Mrs Dale. Was that Mr Ross-Pitt's enormous back I saw disappearing? He's lunching at the house, I expect.'

'Yes, he was in church and walked back this way—he was too early, he said.'

Well, if he didn't hurry he'd be late, reflected Mrs Pettifer. It was natural enough, she supposed, for him to enquire of Henrietta how she was getting on, but she had caught the look on the girl's face, watching him go...

Give him his due, she thought; he would have no idea of the havoc he was causing to Henrietta's feelings—

nor, for that matter, did she have any idea either, which was all right as long as things stayed that way...

'Shall we go over for our dinner? I've looked out some more repairs for you to start on this afternoon.'

Mindful of Mr Ross-Pitt's words, Henrietta took care to avoid Mike Hensen. It was inevitable that they should meet from time to time, but beyond a polite greeting she had nothing to say, and for the next two weeks she took herself off to Thaxted on her day off.

She was still adding to her wardrobe—another blouse, a leather belt, leather gloves since they were going cheap in a sale, sandals, low-heeled and sensible, although she longed to get a pair of high-heeled, strappy ones.

She had joined the library there, too, and carried books back with her, poring over them in the evenings, learning about silver, and antique furniture, paintings and china. By Easter, Mrs Pettifer told Lady Hensen, Henrietta would be quite capable of acting as a house guide.

It was the beginning of April now, and Easter would be very soon. The early mornings were a delight to Henrietta after a lifetime of traffic rumbling and noise.

Now she slipped into the garden with Dickens and Ollie, watching them play as the sun rose higher and listening to the birds. She found it difficult to know one from the other, but she was learning fast. There were squirrels in the trees at the back of the lodge too. Mrs Pettifer said that they were pests, but turned a blind eye when Henrietta put nuts in a convenient hollow, well out of reach of Dickens and Ollie.

She was now able to take long walks on her days off again. Mike Hensen had gone the previous weekend, and although she missed his friendly greetings and obvious pleasure in her company it was a relief not to have to remind herself of Mr Ross-Pitt's words. Despite his charming persuasion, she had refused to go for walks with Mike, and now that he was away she was free to roam where she wanted to.

Besides, it meant that she saved more money—there was a respectable sum in a brown paper bag in the chest of drawers in her room. It wouldn't go far, of course, but she was adding to it as quickly as she could—although she would have to buy some summer dresses.

She had seen Mr Ross-Pitt seldom—his back in church, of course—and he had made no attempt to talk to her since their walk together that Sunday. She avoided that end of the village if she knew he was at home. She had seen Deirdre Stone one day, as she was setting out for her hike, getting out of a car by his house, and Henrietta had hurried quickly away in the opposite direction.

The following week, unaware that Mike Hensen was back again, she met him as she was setting out to walk to Little Bardfield; there was a church there worth visiting, Mrs Pettifer had told her, and Henrietta, drinking in local knowledge like a thirsty flower, was intent on seeing it. There was a bridle path, she was told, which she could follow, and if she was tired she could make the return journey by local bus.

'Not that they run very frequently,' warned Mrs Pettifer, 'but I know there is one around five o'clock; you can ask at the pub.'

Mike Hensen fell in beside her. Back from a few days with friends in the West Country, he was already bored. He had managed to get another week of what he called sick leave but was already regretting that. If it hadn't been for the need to keep on good terms with Sir Peter he would have got into his car and driven back to London.

Here, however, was a chance to while away a few hours. No doubt Henrietta was as bored as he was. He asked her with deceptive casualness where she intended to walk and, when she told him, asked in the nicest possible way if he might go with her. 'I've been staying with friends and I've been longing for some peace and quiet here. The bridle path takes us along the edge of a little wood; there might be bluebells...'

He was careful to talk about nothing much at first, but presently, as she lost her shyness, he began to question her. He put the questions so carefully that she hardly realised them for what they were.

Lady Hensen had never told him much about her and Sir Peter had turned his queries aside. 'Girl's had a rough time of it,' was all he would say, and Mike wanted to know about that rough side. It was easy for him to discover that she had no boyfriend—indeed, had never had one.

'Sweet sixteen and never been kissed,' he said jokingly, and watched the pretty colour creep into her cheeks. He saw her quick frown too, and began to talk about something else. He had thought that she was an insipid girl, more than ready to be flattered and dazzled by him, but now he wasn't so sure. The doubt added interest, though, and he was careful to keep the talk to mundane topics.

At Little Bardfield he invited her to have a sandwich and drink in the pub. 'It's a quiet little place,' he assured her, 'but the church is worth a visit.' He hadn't been into it himself, but it was always safe to say that of a village church.

Henrietta followed him into the pub, her faint uneasiness in his company melting under his casual friendliness. She ate her sandwiches and drank the ginger ale she had asked for and accompanied him across the street to the church. She liked its cool interior and the smell of old wood and candles, and wandered up and down, looking at the memorial plaques on its walls, not noticing how impatient Mike had become. Not that he allowed her to see that.

'We could wait and get the bus back,' he told her, 'but if you're game we could walk back—there's a short cut which will bring us back onto the bridle path.'

The short cut was actually a long one, taking them well away from the bridle path, but Mike was talking amusingly, telling her droll tales of people he had met, and she hardly noticed where they were going, until presently she asked, 'Oughtn't we to be back on the bridle path by now? It seems ages...'

They were following a narrow path beside a hedge; the field was ploughed and something was growing there, and as far as she could see the hedge went on for miles.

'Ages?' Mike laughed and caught her arm. 'My dear girl, when I'm with you time flies.'

Henrietta, not having had the benefit of a normal girl's upbringing, looked startled. 'Whatever do you mean...Mr Hensen? We haven't exchanged half a dozen words since I saw you at Mrs Tibbs'. Actually, I shouldn't be with you—you know that. I've enjoyed our walk, but it's time for me to go back, so perhaps we could hurry a bit.'

'You really mean it, don't you? You're a green girl, aren't you?' He caught hold of her and bent to kiss her. She turned her face away, though, and the kiss landed on her hair. That annoyed him; it looked as though he wasn't going to have his little bit of fun after all. She was only a servant; she should be delighted at having been noticed…

'Let me go,' said Henrietta in a fierce voice. 'At once.' She sounded like an irate schoolmistress.

'You're behaving like a little nun—perhaps you were educated in a convent. Although servants aren't usually educated.'

He was still holding her, and she kicked him smartly on the shin with the toe of her sensible lace-up shoe.

'Nicely placed,' said a well-remembered voice. 'Just wait a tick while I get through this infernal hedge.' Mr Ross-Pitt thrust his way between its branches, followed by the faithful Watson. He said lightly, 'I should like to see myself in the light of an heroic rescuer, but I see that you are coping very nicely, Henrietta.'

He flung a large arm round her shoulders. 'You'd better make yourself scarce, Mike, before I forget my manners. If it is of interest to you, Henrietta was educated in a children's home—a little world of its own where the young had little chance of learning about the wicked ways of our world.'

'It's none of your business—'

'There you are wrong. Henrietta, we will walk back together, with your permission.'

Still with his heavy arm on her shoulders, he walked her away, not looking at her and ignoring Mike, who stood irresolute, white with rage. Mr Ross-Pitt had really treated him like a silly boy, and he'd get even with him for that. What was more, he'd take care to see that Henrietta was sent packing.

Mr Ross-Pitt must have read his thoughts, for he turned round and said, 'By the way, I shouldn't go telling tales to Lady Hensen. It would do no good, you know; and if I find you annoying Henrietta again I shall make mincemeat of you.'

He urged Henrietta along with a firm hand, whistled
to Watson, and set off along the path. He didn't look at
her—a good thing, for she was doing her best not to cry.
'Fortunate that Watson and I chose to come this way for
a walk,' he observed casually. 'Has he been bothering
you much?'

She found her voice. 'No—no, I haven't seen Mr
Hensen much for the last three weeks, and I believe he's
been away with friends for the past week. He—he met
me in the village and said he was walking to Little
Bardfield and wanted to see the church—'

'You haven't been out and about very much, have
you, Henrietta?' His voice was gentle.

'Well, no.' She sounded suddenly snappish. 'It wasn't
encouraged at the children's home, and I—after that I
never had time.'

He said soothingly, 'No, no, of course you didn't. But
don't go walking with anyone unless you're sure they're
your friend.'

She said in a watery voice, 'But I'm walking with
you—I didn't even say I'd come...'

'Ah, yes, but I'm your friend.' He felt in a pocket and
produced a beautifully laundered handkerchief. 'Here,
give a good blow.'

It might have been a kindly uncle or big brother talking, if she had had either; his reassuring normality did
much to restore her spirits. She did as she had been told,
muttering her thanks, and presently said, 'I'm sorry I've
been such a fool. I'm glad you came... You always do!'

'Yes, but only by chance. Don't count on me,
Henrietta.'

The path ended presently and they crossed a stile and
found themselves in a high-banked lane. 'Not far,' said
Mr Ross-Pitt. 'We'll be in nice time for tea.'

Henrietta stood still. 'No, no—I mean, thank you very

much, but I won't come to tea.' She studied his placid face. 'You see, it wouldn't do—it would be the same as going for walks with Mr Hensen, if you understand what I mean. I'm what he said—a servant—'

'Shall we ignore Mr Hensen? You are not a servant, Henrietta, and, even if you were, what is so wrong with that? I am also a servant in my profession, am I not?' He bent suddenly and kissed her cheek. 'Now, be a good girl and rid your head of nonsense and come and have tea with me. Mrs Patch was only saying this morning that she hadn't seen you.'

Which somehow made things perfectly clear.

Mrs Patch was pleased to see her. She made no comment on Henrietta's slightly pink nose, nor did she remark upon Mr Ross-Pitt's handkerchief hanging from her jacket pocket. All she said was, 'Well, here's a sight for sore eyes—how well you look; I can see you're happy up at the house.'

She bustled off to the kitchen. 'Tea in five minutes,' she assured them. Which gave Henrietta time to do something about her face and tidy her hair.

She peered into the cloakroom looking-glass and longed to be beautiful, and she touched with a gentle fingertip the spot where Mr Ross-Pitt had kissed her.

Mrs Patch produced hot buttered toast, fairy cakes, tiny sandwiches and what she described smugly as 'one of my cakes', still smelling faintly of the oven and stuffed with currants and sultanas and chopped nuts. Henrietta ate everything she was offered; lunch had been a long time ago and, anyway, she preferred not to think of it.

She sat opposite Mr Ross-Pitt, with Watson on the rug between them, and wished that she could stay there for ever.

That wasn't possible, of course. She finished her tea,

and in answer to his quiet questions told him about mending the curtains and cleaning the chandeliers and how kind Mrs Pettifer was and how she liked the people with whom she worked. She told him about Dickens and Ollie too, and about the little bird with a nest at the bottom of the garden. 'Quite high in one of the trees, too high for Dickens…'

'Why Dickens?' asked Mr Ross-Pitt, amused at this conversation.

'Well, it was in the market. I was buying some fruit and he was sitting on a pile of sacks behind the stall, and Mr Spink, who owned the stall, hadn't seen him until he turned round, and he said, "What the Dickens?" No one wanted him so I took him back with me and called him Dickens.'

Mr Ross-Pitt laughed. 'He's a fine cat,' he said kindly, 'and Ollie will grow up just as fine, I dare say. Perhaps…' He didn't get any further because the phone rang and he got up to answer it.

When he said, 'Deirdre,' Henrietta got up, murmuring that she would get her jacket, and slipped out of the room. To listen to him talking to Miss Stone was something she didn't wish to do, although she wasn't sure why. The call was brief and he followed her into the hall. 'Sorry about that—I'll drive you back.'

'It's only a short walk and such a fine evening. I've taken up all your afternoon.'

'I'll drive you back, Henrietta. If it makes you more comfortable, I have to see Sir Peter about a small matter.'

She sat beside him in the car, with Watson on the back seat, and because she thought that he was relieved to be rid of her she was silent, anxious on her part not to annoy him further. She watched his large, well-kept hands on the wheel and thought how capable they were—thoroughly dependable, like the man...

She hoped that Deirdre Stone, once she was married to him, would look after him and love him. She gave a little gasping breath; never mind the hateful Deirdre, thought Henrietta, in a sudden overwhelming flash of awareness; it's me who loves him!

'What's the matter?' asked Mr Ross-Pitt without looking at her.

'Nothing, nothing at all,' said Henrietta wildly.

'You sounded as though you had just had a disturbing thought.'

Which was true, but not to be mentioned. At the lodge she skipped out of the car, thanked him in a breathless manner for her tea and his help, and nipped smartly indoors.

Mrs Pettifer was already home. 'Got a lift back?' she asked kindly, and peered at Henrietta's troubled face. 'You're upset. Do you want to tell me?' She paused. 'Not Mr Ross-Pitt?'

'No. Oh, no, he's been so kind; he always is—I mean, I didn't realise... I thought Mr Hensen—he said he wanted to see the church...'

'Sit down, Henrietta, and tell me what has happened...but first I'll make us a cup of cocoa.'

So Henrietta collected her thoughts and gave a blow-by-blow account of her day off. 'And perhaps Mr Hensen will complain about me and I'll get the sack. He—he was so angry because Mr Ross-Pitt treated him as though he was a silly boy.'

'Which he is. Don't worry, my dear; Mike Hensen wants to keep on good terms with his uncle and aunt—he won't risk annoying them. They would be very annoyed if they knew. Besides, Mr Ross-Pitt is quite capable of knocking him down. A quiet man is our Mr

Ross-Pitt, but what he says he means. I think you will find that Mike Hensen keeps well away from you in future.'

'I should never have gone with him.'

'No, you shouldn't, but I can see that it would have been awkward for you to have refused his company. Besides, you had no idea that he was going to behave badly. My fault—I should have warned you.' She smiled suddenly. 'I wish I had seen Mr Ross-Pitt coming through the hedge. Did Mrs Patch give you a good tea?'

They had their supper presently and Henrietta, convinced that she would lie awake half the night, went to bed and was asleep in two minutes. She woke once in the night and remembered in a sudden rush that she loved Adam. It would have to be a secret, of course, and she must contrive not to see him, but there was nothing to stop her from thinking about him and thinking of him as 'Adam'.

She accompanied Mrs Pettifer up to the house the next morning, feeling nervous, but halfway through the morning as they drank their elevenses in the kitchen with the rest of the staff she heard the housekeeper telling Cook that Mr Mike had gone off to London early that morning.

'Said he felt fit enough to do some work and he wouldn't be down for a bit. Not like him, I must say; I wouldn't have said he was one to do an honest day's work if he could get along without it. Going to India, too.'

Feathers hushed her in a dignified way. 'It's not for the likes of us to criticise our betters,' he pointed out severely. 'Not but what you've the right of it.'

When Henrietta had gone upstairs, obedient to Mrs Pettifer's request that she should go up to the linen room and fetch down some frilled pillowcases which needed

careful darning, Mrs Pettifer told them about Mr Mike
Hensen and Henrietta.

'She's not like these modern girls—well, what do you
expect, brought up in a children's home and then living
hand to mouth in an attic?' Her audience nodded sym-
pathetically for they all knew Henrietta's history. 'A
blessing it was that Mr Ross-Pitt turned up just when he
was needed most. Took her back to his place for tea and
drove her back to the lodge. He's a kind man if ever
there was one—wouldn't harm a fly.'

There was general agreement at this. 'It behoves us,'
said Feathers with great dignity, 'to keep an eye on
Henrietta, in a friendly way as it were. I'm sure as how
we all wish her well.'

There was a chorus of assent, for she was liked. Had
she not listened with sympathetic patience to Mrs Dale's
grumbles about running a big house with insufficient
staff, run untold errands for Cook when her feet were
bad, taken letters to the post for Feathers, lent one of the
housemaids a pound so that she could send a birthday
card to her granny—the birthday falling awkwardly just
before pay day—and spent the whole evening searching
for the kitchen cat and found her shut up in the laundry
room?

'Just let anyone bother the girl and I'll give him what
for,' observed Cook sternly, and was answered by an
assertive chorus.

Henrietta, unaware of everyone's concern for her well-
being, quickly settled down to work again. There was
no sign of Mike Hensen, and very soon she stopped
peering round doors before entering a room or hesitating
about answering bells in case he had returned unexpect-
edly. Life resumed its even flow—plenty of work, but

good food and a comfortable bed and her wages each week. And her memories of Mr Ross-Pitt.

Even if she never saw him again, and probably she wouldn't—not to speak of, at any rate—she had those, and the best memory of all was the gentle kiss on her cheek. Sometimes she remembered Mr Hensen's attempts to kiss her too, but she had only to think of Mr Ross-Pitt to forget that entirely.

So on the whole she was happy. Sooner or later Adam would marry, and she would have to get over that as best she could, but until then she allowed her thoughts to dwell upon him and treasured every crumb of information she heard about him. That wasn't much for he was a very private man despite his friendly manner.

This was a sentiment echoed by Deirdre who, despite determined effort, had been unable to coax another invitation to spend a few days at Mr Ross-Pitt's home out of him. She had contrived to meet him fairly frequently, badgering her mother to find out from her friends and acquaintances when and where he might be dining with mutual friends and then scheming to be invited.

He had been friendly on these occasions but that was all; questions put to him concerning his private life he'd evaded with easy good humour, and her delicate hints that they might meet more frequently had been met with a bland politeness. If only she could engage his attention—catch his eye. Chic new outfits had no effect upon him at all; he might compliment her on her appearance, but she felt sure that he really had no idea what she was wearing or how well turned out she was.

She could have saved herself a good deal of time and money if she had known that he regarded her with indifference nicely concealed by good manners, while if he thought about her appearance at all it was to compare it unfavourably with Henrietta's sober attire. Not that this prevented him from picturing Henrietta in more attractive and colourful garments—she would look nice in anything, even an old sack.

These observations, he told himself, were merely the outcome of a natural interest in her welfare. It was to be hoped that she would meet some worthy young man and settle down, then perhaps he would be rid of her image popping up with increasing frequency to annoy him.

CHAPTER SIX

WITH Easter a week away now, Henrietta was being put through her paces as a guide. Each day Mrs Pettifer led her round the vast rooms which would be open to the public, reciting their contents and making her repeat them until she was word perfect. There was the ballroom, the vast drawing room seldom used by the family, the banqueting room—'Never used at all,' said Mrs Pettifer in an aside, 'except for weddings, christenings and funerals'—the main hall and the great staircase which led them to the only two bedrooms on view, both with canopied beds, vast wardrobes and Hepplewhite dressing tables with their giltwood toilet mirrors, and Regency day-beds and giltwood chairs.

The second bedroom contained a leather screen— Dutch painted leather, eighteenth century and worth a small fortune—'And don't forget the ormolu clock on the side-table—French, Louis XV,' said Mrs Pettifer. 'Pierre Leroy made it, just in case anyone asks. They seldom do. The carpet in this room is an Aubusson and in the other bedroom a Tabriz, but you already know that, for you helped me to clean them, didn't you?'

By the end of the week Henrietta was a bundle of nerves. The house was to open on Easter Monday and she spent her usual Sunday afternoon sitting in the office, becoming more and more nervous—a state of mind Mrs Pettifer cured by coming over to the house before supper.

'I'm a visitor,' she told Henrietta. 'Take me round the

house. Don't worry, there's no one about and it's a splendid chance for you to rehearse.'

Henrietta, very much on her mettle now, led Mrs Pettifer from room to room, trying to pretend that the lady was a group of interested tourists and succeeding very well.

'Well done,' said Mrs Pettifer. 'You'll be all right— remember that visitors have come to see the inside of the house and its contents, not you.'

A most successful day, Lady Hensen assured Mrs Pettifer as the last of the tourists trooped down the drive. She had been presiding at the counter in the garden room, turned into a café for the occasion. 'We did really well in the tearoom. It always surprises me that so many people want to see round the place. Did Henrietta manage? No gaffes?'

'None. She is going to be very satisfactory. She's intelligent and keen and she wants to know about everything she sees and does.'

'Splendid. She will be capable of guiding each afternoon, you think?'

'Oh, perfectly, Lady Hensen. You don't want her day off altered? She has Tuesday.'

'Why don't we let her have Saturday? She has Sunday morning, doesn't she? That will give her a nice break; she could even stay away if she wanted to for the night.'

Mrs Pettifer said bleakly, 'She has nowhere to go, Lady Hensen.'

'No, no, of course not. How silly of me. Has she made any friends in the village?'

'Well, they all know her—she's well liked there and she visits Mrs Tibbs sometimes—but friends, no...' Mrs Pettifer frowned. 'She's shy and reserved although she's so well liked—she takes an interest in everyone, you see, asks after their rheumatism and the baby and where they're going for their holidays, and she is really interested and they know it. But she never talks about herself.'

'She's happy?'

'Oh, yes, and an undemanding companion; I have grown quite fond of her. May I tell her that you're pleased with her, Lady Hensen, and ask if she would like to have Saturday free? She'll be acting as a guide for the rest of the week?'

'Yes, I dare say the two of you will be able to manage between you for most of the time; Mrs Bruce—the vicar's wife—will do Saturday afternoons with you and come in on Wednesdays if she's needed; that's our busy day, isn't it?'

Henrietta went pink with pleasure when Mrs Pettifer passed on Lady Hensen's satisfaction. 'And she has decided,' added Mrs Pettifer, 'that you shall have Saturday for your free day so that you get a nice long break until Sunday afternoon. You're pleased?'

'Yes, thank you. But you'll still get your day off, won't you?'

'Yes, of course, child. Monday is usually very quiet and I'm free on Tuesday morning now; that gives me a long break too.'

Mrs Pettifer settled down with Ollie on her lap. 'Now, tell me, what did you think of the visitors? Did they ask questions? Sometimes you can do the whole tour and nobody asks a thing.'

Henrietta reflected. 'I was rather surprised that no one asked about the screen—it's so beautiful. There was an elderly lady who wanted to know about the clocks, but the third group I took round didn't say anything, only when we went downstairs again someone wanted to know where they could get tea...'

Mrs Pettifer laughed. 'We get all sorts, and just now and again along comes someone who's really interested, and that is deeply satisfying for us.'

By the time Saturday came, Henrietta was more than glad of a free day. The spate of visitors over Easter had dwindled to a steady trickle—enough to keep her or Mrs Pettifer busy during the afternoons—and in the mornings there was no let up over her usual chores.

The rooms had to be kept in a pristine state, dusted and vacuumed and checked to make sure that everything was still there. There were always odds and ends left behind by forgetful visitors—plastic bags, bottles of lemonade, the occasional half-eaten sandwich, scarves. Any items of clothing had to be collected up, labelled with the date and put into a box in case the various owners came in search of them.

Getting ready to go out on Saturday morning, Henrietta reflected that the week had been fun. She would take herself to Thaxted, have lunch in the small café that she had discovered previously and do a round of the shops. She would soon need something more summery—a plain navy blue skirt and another blouse, they would do nicely when she was acting as guide, and later on she could get some woollies for the skirt.

She had her coffee in the quiet little café where she intended to lunch and then began a tour of Thaxted's shops. She was wearing the jersey skirt and jacket and the pastel blouse, and Mr Ross-Pitt, coming out of the corn chandler's shop, stopped to look at her. It was a pity that she wore such dull colours, although he had to admit that she always looked pleasing to the eye.

He crossed the street in a leisurely manner and wished

her good morning, and was quite startled at the rush of colour which flooded her cheeks. But her good morning was uttered in a quiet voice which gave no hint as to the riot of feeling churning around her insides.

'Having a day off?' he wanted to know pleasantly.

'Yes, and as I get Sunday mornings too it's like having a weekend...'

'I dare say you're kept busy with visitors. You are enjoying acting as a guide?'

She wondered how he knew that. 'Yes, very much.' He stood looking down at her, not speaking, so that she felt constrained to say something. 'You're having a day off too?'

'The weekend. Shall we have a cup of coffee and you can tell me how you're getting on?'

'I've just had coffee, thank you.'

'In that case, unless you have something special to do, keep me company. I'm going to visit my mother's old housekeeper; she lives at a small place called Tollesbury on the Essex coast.'

'But she doesn't know me—I mean, a stranger and unexpected.'

'She would be delighted to have company. Matty lives alone—she won't have it otherwise—although she has good neighbours on either side of her and we all visit her frequently. You will like her, Henrietta, and I would be delighted to have company.'

'Isn't Watson with you?'

He laughed. 'Oh, yes, and a splendid listener. Unfortunately he can't answer back.'

She wanted to ask him why his Deirdre wasn't with him but prudence made her hold her tongue. It would be delightful beyond her wildest dreams to spend a few hours in his company. Henrietta got into the car, replied to Watson's delighted greeting with suitable warmth, and

allowed her present happiness to overcome any doubts
she might have in the future concerning the rashness of
her actions.

As for Mr Ross-Pitt, he appeared to have no doubts
at all. His manner was casually friendly as he told her
about the countryside they were driving through, the
towns they would pass and about Tollesbury itself. Once
a fishing village, he explained, but left behind by the
sea, surrounded now by creeks and marshes.

'At the back of beyond, many people say, and I suppose in a sense they are right, although it's only eight
miles from Maldon which is a small town—we go
through it presently. This is Braintree we're running into
now....'

They drove through two other small towns—Witham
and then Heybridge—before bypassing Maldon and taking the road to Tollesbury.

'The sea,' observed Mr Ross-Pitt. 'There's a path—
several paths—through the marshes.'

'The sea,' echoed Henrietta, and craned her neck
round him to see it better.

He was struck by a thought. 'You've seen the sea
before?'

She shook her head. 'No. It's wonderful.' He touched
a switch and the windows rolled down so that she could
sniff the air. 'It's like drinking very clear, cold water and
it smells like heaven.'

He looked at her rapt face and smiled a little. A half-
formed idea crept into the back of his mind, to be forgotten as he rounded a curve and the village came in
sight— Neat cottages, plaster and brick with ancient,
tiled roofs, a village square, a couple of small shops and
a church behind a high stone wall. He pulled up before
one of the cottages and got out, opened her door and

helped her out, released Watson, and thumped the handsome brass knocker.

The door was opened by an old lady, cosily plump with white hair strained back into a tidy bun, and old-fashioned steel spectacles on her small turned-up nose. The spectacles shielded faded blue eyes which twinkled with delight at the sight of them.

'Mr Adam.' She held up her face for his kiss. 'Right on time; you always were a punctual little boy. Come on in, and your little lady...' She beamed at Henrietta, who went red and gave him a reproachful look.

'This is Henrietta Cowper, Matty; she works for Lady Hensen.'

Matty offered a cheek for Henrietta's kiss. 'Now isn't this nice? Come along, my dear; it will be a treat to have a bit of a gossip. You'll need to tidy yourself, no doubt. Such a pretty jacket and skirt...'

The cottage was very small, very clean and nicely furnished. While Mr Ross-Pitt took Watson to the kitchen to give him a drink, Matty led Henrietta up the short, narrow staircase. 'There's the bathroom, dearie; come down when you're ready.' She smiled. 'Such a treat having the pair of you.'

Henrietta didn't hurry; she guessed that Matty might want to question Adam about her and it would make it much easier if she was told at once that Henrietta was with him by casual invitation. When she went downstairs they were in the small living room, one seated each side of the old-fashioned Rayburn, alight even though it was a mild day.

Adam got up as she went in, and pulled up a chair. 'I've been telling Matty about your job,' he told her.

The old lady chimed in, 'Interesting it must be, meeting all sorts of folk, I dare say.'

'Yes, it is, but I help around the house too,' said Henrietta, anxious not to sail under false colours.

'There's pleasure to be got from tending good furniture and silver and such. I don't hold with modern rubbish. Mr Adam says that you worked at his hospital. You liked that, no doubt, but who'd live in London when they can live free and easy, away from all them rows of little houses and smoky factories?' She paused for breath. 'Mr Adam, be so kind as to open that bottle of sherry you so kindly brought with you, and we'll have a drink before I dish up.'

Between them they made Henrietta feel completely at home, sitting at the round table in the little kitchen, eating Matty's steak and kidney pudding, with carrots from a neighbour's garden, and potatoes from the local farmer, who fetched a sack for her whenever they were needed. There was apple pie to follow, with cream from the same farm.

'I may live alone,' said Matty comfortably, 'but there's not a day passes but what someone pops in, and your ma, Mr Adam, telephones without fail each week. She's coming down to see me as soon as that baby's born. How's Miss—Mrs Langley; it's high time, surely?'

'Next week Matty.' He turned to Henrietta. 'My younger sister is having her first baby; my mother is staying with them—they live in Cumbria.' He saw the unspoken questions she wasn't going to ask. 'I've got another sister, married too—she has two boys. My mother and father live on the Northumbrian coast.'

'A long way,' said Henrietta.

'We contrive to see each other quite frequently.' He didn't add to that and presently she helped Matty with the washing-up and set a tray ready for tea, wondering what was to happen next. Should she take herself off for a stroll so that they could talk if they wished?

When she went back into the living room he got to his feet. 'Matty has a nap in the afternoons; we'll take Watson for a brisk walk...'

Matty was still in the kitchen.

'Don't you want to talk? I mean, you came to see her and you might want to say things—I mean, without me there.'

He shook his head. 'Matty needs a rest, especially after the excitement of us coming. After tea you can potter in the kitchen and leave us alone, but only if you feel that you must.'

'Well, yes, I do feel that I must. I hope it hasn't spoilt your visit to her, my being here as well.'

'On the contrary, I fancy she will like to see you again. She's had a long and busy life and she loves to talk about it.'

'It would be lovely to have a granny like her,' said Henrietta. There was no self-pity in her voice, only regret.

A sudden pang of pity made him say briskly, 'Are you ready? We'll take the lane to the marshes. There's a boat yard on one of the creeks; you might like to see that.'

They walked for an hour or so, Henrietta taking great sniffs of sea air and stopping every now and then to stare out to sea, while Watson raced to and fro fetching the sticks Adam threw for him. They didn't talk much.

She was a restful companion, he thought, not fussing about spoiling her shoes or minding that the wind was tossing her hair all over the place. Indeed, he reflected with amusement, she quite forgot him from time to time, bending over a little pool of water or collecting shells and pebbles.

When they turned for home again he observed, 'I

think that you must come here again—an hour or so isn't enough, is it?'

She gave him a rapt look. 'Even if I never come here again, I'll never forget it...'

They had tea with Matty—scones and jam and cream and a dough cake—and when they had finished Henrietta cleared away the tea things and went into the kitchen and shut the door, declaring that it was time she did her share.

Matty looked doubtful. 'There's no need for the child to wash up the tea things; I've all the time in the world.'

'I think Henrietta feels that we might like a little talk together without her. And indeed I should be glad of five minutes alone with you, Matty. There isn't time to tell you about Henrietta; suffice it to say that she had a hard time of it until she got this job at Lady Hensen's place. Believe it or not, she hadn't seen the sea...

'She has a day off on Saturday, and Sunday mornings free; would you consider having her to spend the night just once in a while? The invitation would have to come from you; if she knew it was I who'd suggested it she would refuse at once. She's stiff with pride—understandably. I'll bear expenses, of course, and it will have to be when I have a weekend free. That can be arranged later.'

'There's nothing I'd like better—a bit of company from time to time and a nice chat.' Matty gave him a shrewd look. 'Like her, do you, Mr Adam?'

'She interests me, Matty, and I'd like to see her making a secure future for herself. She's earned it.'

'She's gently bred,' said Matty softly. 'Never mind the clothes—bought to last, I shouldn't wonder, and no money to spare for all the pretty things girls want. Let's hope she meets some good man who'll look after her.'

Mr Ross-Pitt frowned and agreed rather testily.

They got into the car presently and Watson, much

refreshed by a splendid tea after his exercise, sprawled on the back seat and snored gently.

Matty came to the door to see them off. She had kissed Henrietta and pressed a pot of home-made marmalade into her hands. 'I do hope I'll see you again—perhaps we can think of something...'

Henrietta gave her a little hug. 'When I have my holidays perhaps I'll come for the day, if you'll have me?' she said. 'After the tourist season is over.'

She thought about her day as they drove back; Mr Ross-Pitt was silent and she made no attempt to talk; the silence wasn't unfriendly and if he wanted to start a conversation she was quite ready to join in.

Eventually he said, 'Matty is a dear old lady, isn't she? She loves visitors although she says she's never lonely. My mother wanted her to have a cottage close to the house, but she was born around here and she had set her heart on ending her days in Tollesbury. I so wish I could spare the time to see her more often.'

'Has she no family?'

'A very old brother somewhere in Wales. Nephews and nieces in Australia.'

He relapsed into silence once more, and she wondered what he was thinking about. He wasn't anxious exactly, she decided, stealing a loving glance at his profile, but something was making him thoughtful. Perhaps he had a serious operation that he was worried about...

Mr Ross-Pitt never worried about his work—his surgery came to him as naturally as breathing; he might worry about a patient, but never about his skill with a knife. He wasn't worried, only impatient at the thought that he had engaged to take Deirdre out to dinner that evening. That the invitation had been more or less forced upon him by her, good manners making it unavoidable, made the prospect of an evening with her most unpleasing.

He glanced at Henrietta's unassuming profile. She had very long, curling eyelashes. He wondered why he hadn't noticed them before; he hadn't noticed that her small nose had the smallest tilt to it either. A pity it wasn't she he would be dining with...

It was just after six o'clock when he stopped outside the lodge. Henrietta leaned over to say goodbye to Watson and got out when Adam opened her door. She held out a hand. 'Thank you for a lovely day,' she said, and smiled up at him. How tiresome it was to love someone so unobtainable, she thought as she did so, but, never mind, she had a whole day to treasure.

'I enjoyed it too,' said Mr Ross-Pitt, and for a moment she thought that he had more to say, but he shook her hand briefly, got into his car and drove off for all the world as though he had had enough of her. Well, perhaps he had, she reflected, turning her back on the magnificent car and smiling at Mrs Pettifer waiting at the open door.

Henrietta told her about their day over supper, and Mrs Pettifer agreed that it had been very kind of Mr Ross-Pitt to take her to the sea, and kept her thoughts to herself.

Henrietta was a nice girl—just the kind of girl to lose her heart to someone like Adam Ross-Pitt, something which wouldn't do at all. She was sure that he wouldn't dream of encouraging Henrietta in any sentimental notions, but Mrs Pettifer considered that he was a man who wasn't aware of his own power to charm females... Besides, there was this rumour that he was to marry Deirdre Stone.

'Which wouldn't do at all,' said Mrs Pettifer aloud.

A remark which made Henrietta look at her with surprise.

Adam drove himself to London in a thoroughly bad temper. He would, of course, have to suppress it later, but now with only himself to reckon with he could give vent to his annoyance. His weekend was spoilt for a start and, heaven knew, he didn't get one very often. To take his mind off the evening ahead of him he pulled over to the side of the road, picked up the car phone and rang his registrar, who told him in some surprise that to date there was nothing urgent.

'I thought you'd be buried in your village,' he observed.

'So did I—unfortunately I've had to come back to town to keep an engagement. I'll give you the number of the restaurant. You'll know where I am if you should need another pair of hands.'

'Let's hope not. Burrows has just rung to say he won't be available—his small daughter's come down with measles despite her jabs.'

'You've got a couple of housemen lined up for Accident and Emergency, Peter?'

'Yes. As long as it's only the usual Saturday night rush we'll be OK.'

Adam drove on, threaded his way through the City and the West End and stopped before a house in Chelsea. He was admitted by a sulky-looking maid and shown upstairs to the drawing room where Deirdre was waiting for him. 'Adam—how lovely to see you—it seems ages. Mother's gone to play bridge.' She came and stood close to him. 'Shall we have a drink before we go?'

He glanced at his watch. 'I booked a table for eight o'clock; I think we had better go.'

She pouted and then smiled. 'Very well. We can talk

over dinner. Have you had a busy week? It must be good for you to enjoy an evening away from all that illness and those dreary wards.'

They went out to the car and he found her perfume overpowering. Henrietta, he reflected, had smelled of the sea and a faint whiff of shampoo and soap...

Deirdre took a long time deciding what she would eat, querying each dish as she did so. 'I have to be so careful of my diet,' she told Adam. 'I've always been fussy with food.'

He wondered if she had ever been really hungry as she picked delicately at a lobster claw.

He was called to the phone halfway through their noisettes of lamb. His senior registrar's apologetic voice said, 'I feel awful dragging you away from what must be a delightful evening; we've been inundated—there's been some sort of fracas. The CO asked me to take a look at some of the casualties and there is one whom I'd like you to see. I've had him X-rayed—a depressed fracture of the base of the skull—blow with a pickaxe seems likely. There's a fragment lodged in the temporal lobe.'

'I'll be with you in fifteen minutes.' Adam went back to his table. Deirdre was still nibbling at her lamb and she looked up as he reached it.

'What a tiresome life you do lead, Adam,' she said playfully. 'I can see that someone will have to alter your ways—being interrupted in the middle of dinner indeed...' She smiled up at him, and then said sharply, 'Well, sit down, do—I'm bored on my own.'

'I'm afraid I must go—that was the hospital. I'm sorry, Deirdre. I'll see the *maître d'* as I leave. Please finish your dinner—he'll get a taxi for you.'

She was furious. 'I'm expected to stay here on my

own?' Her voice had grown shrill with temper. 'The least you can do is drive me home—'

'While I am doing that a patient might die,' he reminded her quietly. 'I'm afraid this is one of the hazards of spending an evening with a member of the medical profession. Do please forgive me.'

She was white with a rage that she was trying to contain. 'I can see that it is certainly high time that someone took you in hand, Adam; you need a wife.'

He didn't answer that but wished her goodbye, had a word with the *maître d'* and went out to his car. The streets were comparatively quiet; he was at the hospital only a short time after the fifteen minutes he had promised and Peter was waiting for him.

Once he'd examined the man he decided to operate. 'For the man hasn't a chance otherwise, and it will be touch and go as it is. Tell Theatre, will you? I'll be up in ten minutes.'

He had no other thought but his work for the next few hours, and when at last the man was wheeled away to Intensive Care he was surprised to find that it was past midnight—too late to drive home. He decided to stay the night at his flat, see his patient early in the morning and then go home for the rest of Sunday.

It was barely six o'clock when Mr Ross-Pitt left the hospital the next morning. His patient was holding his own and there was nothing more to be done for the time being. He drove through the quiet Sunday streets and out of London into early-morning sunshine, and presently there were green fields and trees. There was almost no traffic; he was unlocking his door an hour later, to be greeted by Watson's cheerful bark and Mrs Patch's voice.

'There you are, Mr Adam. We were beginning to

wonder what had happened to you.' She gave him a sharp glance as she came into the hall, but she smiled with relief when she saw him. He'd been up half the night; she'd seen that look on his face before—not enough sleep and concerned for whoever it was. She wondered what had happened to Miss Stone—he had told her that he was taking her out to dinner...

She said now, 'I'll have breakfast on the table by the time you're showered and changed. Eggs and bacon, mushrooms, tomatoes...'

'A couple of sausages? I had to miss most of dinner.'

'Bless the man—and a nice slice of fried bread?'

'I'll be ten minutes.' He whistled to Watson and went up to his room and came down presently, wearing well-cut tweeds and a tie.

'Church?' asked Mrs Patch, laying a piled-up plate before him.

'Yes—it's my turn to read the lesson.'

He walked Watson before walking to church. He saw Henrietta at once, sitting in her usual pew at the back of the church, but she was listening to old Mr Pike from the almshouses and didn't see him. After the service, he promised himself, they might walk back together.

By the time he reached the church porch on the way out she had disappeared, and he walked back feeling vaguely disappointed. He would have liked to have told her about his long night—a notion which surprised him, for he seldom talked about his work, but the memory of their day together with Matty still lingered and he wanted to see her again.

She had seen him, of course, and had slipped away and out sight, fearful that if she lingered she might look as though she was imposing on his good nature after their day together. It was a good thing that there were more visitors than usual in the afternoon, so that she had no time to think about him.

It was in the kitchen, having a late tea after the last tourist had been ushered out, that Henrietta heard Cook telling Feathers that Mr Ross-Pitt had been seen arriving home just after seven o'clock in the morning. 'And I did hear from Mrs Patch that he was dining with that Miss Stone in London. Looks as though there'll be wedding bells, don't it? Out all night...'

Feathers said repressively, 'That is something we don't know, Cook. I do not think that Mr Ross-Pitt would disport himself in an ungentlemanly fashion, even with the young lady he intends to marry. I think it more likely that he was engaged at the hospital.'

Henrietta hoped Feathers was right, but Deirdre had to be reckoned with. She was after all, good-looking, well dressed and shared the same lifestyle as Mr Ross-Pitt. At least, she did when he wasn't at the hospital or seeing patients. She would make a bride to be proud of, in white—no, not white, she wasn't young enough for that—in cream satin and someone's priceless old lace veil, and she would know just how to behave.

Indeed, thought Henrietta, trying to be fair, she would make a splendid wife for an eminent surgeon, knowing all the right people and holding intimate dinner parties and wearing the right clothes.

I hate her, thought Henrietta, sitting there listening to the kitchen gossip.

Since it was Mrs Pettifer's day off on Monday, Henrietta got up early, saw to the needs of Dickens and Ollie, took her a cup of tea and got her own breakfast before going up to the house.

There was plenty of work waiting for her—polishing the fine old furniture, rubbing up some of the silver, running to and fro with tea and sugar and milk for the ladies getting ready for the teas that they would serve that afternoon—and Henrietta, who had learnt that work was an antidote to many of the less pleasant things in life, was glad to be kept busy.

Nevertheless, she couldn't prevent Mr Ross-Pitt's handsome visage dancing before her eyes from time to time. It was a pity that there was only a bare handful of visitors in the afternoon. She would have welcomed a crowd to distract her thoughts.

There was no sign of him during the week, although Feathers mentioned at dinner one day that Sir Peter and Lady Hensen were dining with him on the following evening.

On Saturday Henrietta took herself off to Saffron Walden—further away than Thaxted, but larger and with more shops, Mrs Pettifer had said. Since the days were warmer and summer wasn't far off, she decided to find the skirt and blouse that she had intended to get when she had met Mr Ross-Pitt, and perhaps a pretty dress...

The shops were all that Mrs Pettifer had said and Henrietta loved the town; she would have to come again, she promised herself before she began her shopping.

She found a skirt almost at once—finely pleated and of thin material in a sober navy blue; she found two blouses too, short-sleeved and neatly collared, after which sensible choice she ignored prudence and bought a sage-green dress in cotton—the saleslady described it as a safari dress—but Henrietta could see that it would pass muster for any occasion during the day.

Not that she expected to lead a social life, but just supposing Matty should ask her to visit her again? And there was church on Sundays. A good investment, she told herself, and five minutes later succumbed to a simply cut floral dress, so plain that it wouldn't date. It was uncrushable too, said the friendly saleslady—just right for taking on holiday.

Henrietta thought it unlikely that she would have a holiday, but she didn't say so. Perhaps a day out later on, when her nest egg had swollen to sufficient proportions...

Mr Ross-Pitt was in church on Sunday, but beyond a friendly nod he had nothing to say to her. She hadn't expected it, but all the same she felt a pang of disappointment, instantly suppressed; loving him couldn't be avoided, but encouraging her love would do no good at all. Perhaps it would be a good thing if she didn't go to church, she thought, but that was something she didn't want to miss. She might only be on nodding terms with other people in the congregation but it made her feel that she belonged and she enjoyed singing the hymns.

At the back of her head was the vague idea that if Deirdre Stone were to marry him and come to live in the village then she—Henrietta—wouldn't be able to bear to live there too. There had been no more gossip about them in the kitchen, though, so perhaps it had been just that—gossip!

It surprised her that the staff at the manor knew so much about everyone living in the village, and although she didn't pay much heed to it she did listen when Cook remarked over coffee the next morning that Mr Mike Hensen was in India.

'Gone on a long holiday, I heard Sir Peter telling Mr Ross-Pitt when he was here the other evening. There's some talk about Sir Peter and Lady Hensen going to the States to visit Miss Trudy—expecting again, I hear—and her husband away so much.'

'Hearsay, Cook,' said Feathers loftily. 'If this is true then we shall be informed at the proper time.'

No more was said and the days slipped by, bringing their quota of visitors and polishing, dusting and mending. If it hadn't been for the fact that, try as she might, Henrietta couldn't rid herself of Mr Ross-Pitt's vast image, she would have been completely happy.

It was at Sunday midday dinner that Feathers made his announcement. 'Sir Peter and Lady Hensen will be travelling to the States in ten days' time. The house is to be closed for a period of two weeks. We are each of us to have one week of our annual holiday, and for reasons of security I shall remain for the first week with Agnes, Cook and Henrietta. On the following week Mrs Dale, Mrs Pettifer and you, Addy, and Maud—' he nodded at the kitchen maid '—will return here. You may remember Fletcher, who left when he married—he will be here for the two weeks, and Jimmy—the gardener's elder son—will do the same.'

There was a ripple of excitement and everyone began to talk at once. Roast beef forgotten on their plates, they started making their plans. It was Mrs Pettifer who said quietly to Henrietta, 'You can stay at the lodge for the two weeks—take day trips during your holiday and look after yourself and the cats. You won't mind being alone while I'm away?'

Henrietta said, 'Of course not,' rather too quickly, but she smiled widely and they all nodded and smiled back, relieved that she would be content.

'A pity the child hasn't somewhere to go,' said Mrs Pettifer as she drank a last cup of tea with the housekeeper.

CHAPTER SEVEN

MR ROSS-PITT, informed of the happenings at the manor a week later, ate his dinner and allowed his thoughts free rein. There was no reason, he told himself, why he should bother with Henrietta. She was quite happy where she was. All the same, later that evening, working at his desk, he put down his pen and reached for the phone.

Henrietta gave a good deal of thought to her holiday; to go away was out of the question—she couldn't afford it; besides, where would she go? Addy was going to a Butlins camp with her boyfriend. 'It's grand,' she told Henrietta. 'Lots of fun, you know—dancing and concerts and such—never a dull moment.' She frowned. 'But I don't know as how I'd like to go on me own.'

Mrs Pettifer had a sister living in Wiltshire, Cook had a brother in Clapham Common; everyone had somewhere to go, but they were careful not to talk too much about it when Henrietta was there.

There wasn't much leisure to talk anyway; several of the rooms were to be closed while the Hensens were away, rooms had to be got ready for the two men who were coming to stay, luggage had to be brought down from the vast attics and Cook was busy filling the freezer so that those left behind could be properly fed in her absence.

The house seemed very quiet two weeks later as Henrietta went to her dinner after seeing Mrs Pettifer on her way. Feathers handed her a letter as she sat down.

'For me? I don't know anyone...' She looked at the postmark, but it was faint and smudged.

'Open it and see,' someone suggested.

It was from Matty, penned in a spidery hand. She had written:

It would be nice to see you again. I wonder if you get any holidays? If you do, would you consider coming here for a few days and keeping me company? I don't go out much and you would be welcome any time. I expect you're busy now the tourist season is starting, but I thought I'd write just in case you get a few days off. Perhaps you've already made arrangements, and it might be dull for you here, but I would dearly like the company!

Henrietta read the letter through once more and then glanced up at the faces watching her. 'It's from an old lady who lives at Tollesbury. I—I met her a little while ago...' She had better explain about Mr Ross-Pitt, she thought, and they all listened, nodding and smiling, just as though it were news to them. Long since, Mrs Pettifer had told them all about her visit to the old lady but no one said a word, only expressed delight at this unexpected treat coming Henrietta's way.

Feathers spoke. 'If this lady is on the telephone you may ring from here, Henrietta, and arrange to go and see her. That is if you wish to go.'

'Oh, I do, Mr Feathers. It was wonderful—do you suppose I could go for the whole week? Would that be too long?'

'Certainly not. I gather that the lady lives alone?'

'Yes. She is elderly, but she isn't lonely, I think.'

'You will be a new face, someone fresh to talk to. Eat

your dinner and then go and telephone. You may use the one in the office.'

Matty's old voice sounded pleased. 'Come for as long as you like. You'll have to catch a bus and change, but I'll be here waiting for you—Saturday, you said? A whole week of company. I'll enjoy that, my dear. You won't find it dull?'

'Dull? Oh, Matty, no. I can't wait to see you and the sea, and the marshes.'

Matty put the phone down and then picked it up again. Mr Adam might say that his only interest in Henrietta was to see that she had a bit of a holiday, but Matty knew better even if he didn't.

Henrietta had worked out how to get to Tollesbury—bus to Braintree, bus to Maldon and then another bus. An awkward journey, but she would have only a weekend bag with her and she would start out early in the morning. She didn't like leaving Dickens and Ollie, although she knew that they would be well cared for by the rest of the staff. They were happy and contented, though, secure and well fed, sure of a willing lap to curl up on.

She packed her two new dresses, a cardigan, a couple of blouses, crammed in her quilted jacket, bade goodbye to Dickens and Ollie, and, seen off by Feathers, went down to the village to catch the early morning bus.

History repeated itself. She hadn't been standing at the bus stop for more than a minute when Mr Ross-Pitt drew up beside her. His good morning was uttered with just the right amount of pleasant surprise. 'Off on your travels?' he wanted to know.

She turned a beaming face to his, delighted to see him, if only for a moment. 'Matty has invited me to go and stay with her.'

His look of surprise seemed genuine; he should have been an actor.

'Matty? But I'm on my way to see her! I've managed a free day and I thought I'd surprise her. That's splendid.' He got out of the car and picked up her bag, put it in the boot and opened the car door. 'We'll be there in time for coffee.'

She hesitated, oblivious of the interested faces turned in their direction. 'Oh, but if you're going—I mean, I could go tomorrow...'

'You prefer not to be seen with me?'

'Don't be ridiculous, Mr Ross-Pitt. You know what I mean; Matty might like to have you to herself.'

The bus creeping up behind them settled the matter. Mr Ross-Pitt tossed her into the car, bade the queue good morning, waved to the bus driver and got in beside her. 'I have never met such a girl for arguing,' he observed mildly.

Watson poked a friendly nose between them, and she put up a hand to stroke him. 'Well, at least you are civil to him,' said Mr Ross-Pitt.

'Civil? Of course I'm civil,' began Henrietta, still smarting from the indignity of being shoved into the car, however gently. 'You didn't ask me if I wanted to come.' Her ill humour suddenly left her. 'I'm sorry, I didn't mean a word of that; it's just that I was taken by surprise.'

'Good. You can come off your high horse and tell me how you managed to get a holiday.'

He listened to her explaining, knowing all about it anyway, but expressing interest and surprise with just the right degree of attention. 'Matty will be delighted,' he observed. 'You'll be trotted round the village to visit her friends. How long are you staying?' He sounded casual.

'Until next Saturday. I have to be back by six o'clock in the evening.'

'I'll fetch you, and before you think of any number of reasons why I shouldn't I must tell you that I had already planned to visit Matty next weekend. There are some papers she must sign; I shall leave them with her today.'

Which sounded reasonable enough to Henrietta.

They were given a warm welcome when they reached Matty's little house.

'Well, isn't this just lovely?' she exclaimed. 'Seeing you again, Henrietta, and now Mr Adam coming so unexpected-like. There's coffee ready and waiting, and a seed cake. Come along in, do.'

He didn't stay long; he took Henrietta's bag upstairs to the little bedroom over the porch, drank his coffee and ate most of the cake and then, while Henrietta tactfully went upstairs to unpack, had his talk with Matty.

Whatever it was about it had made the old lady very cheerful, she reflected when she went downstairs again, just in time to thank Mr Ross-Pitt and wish him goodbye. They stood at the door and waved until he was out of sight and she hugged the happy thought to herself that she would see him again in a week's time.

The week which followed was one which she knew she would never forget. Matty might have been old, but she had the heart and brain of a girl concealed by the manner of an ideal granny. She had no difficulty in getting Henrietta to tell her about her childhood and rather dreary upbringing, her efforts to make a life for herself and her lack of money.

'What a good thing that Mr Adam should have stumbled over you,' she observed, and, seeing the colour creep into Henrietta's cheeks, went on chattily, 'And even better that Lady Hensen wanted help at the manor. One thing leads to another, and just think, if he hadn't seen you in Thaxted and brought you here with him I might never have known you.'

'Or I you,' said Henrietta. 'It's so—so comforting, if you see what I mean, having someone. I don't know how to say it…'

Matty patted her arm. 'No need, dearie; I understand exactly how you feel. Now, if you're ready, we'll pop across the square and see if Mrs Watkins has got that wool I ordered. I knit the thick socks Mr Adam wears inside his rubber boots. Very careless he is about looking after himself properly. He needs a wife.'

Henrietta very nearly told Matty about Deirdre Stone then, but she stopped herself just in time. It was none of her business, and probably Matty knew about her anyway.

She learned a great deal about his family in those days. His mother was a fine lady, said Matty, and so kind and thoughtful of everyone. His father too—he'd been a surgeon but now he had retired. They lived in the north—the coast of Northumberland—in a fine house. She heard about his sisters too; Matty was a fount of knowledge, although she didn't gossip. Obviously she was a loyal and devoted servant to the family and always would be.

Each afternoon Matty retired to her room to have what she called 'a little lay down' and Henrietta roamed the surrounding countryside and seashore until teatime. The weather, while not high summer, was pleasantly warm even when it rained, and she went most days across the marshes down to the sea, but once or twice she found her way to the small shipyard on one of the creeks, and the men working there told her to feel free to look around her. They took time off to explain their work to her and told her that she was welcome to go again whenever she wished.

She and Matty had been to the vicarage to tea one afternoon and there she had met the vicar's eldest son, an earnest young man at a theological college. David was astonished to hear that she walked down to the shore. 'It's quite a distance,' he pointed out, 'even if you take the path along the estuary.'

'It's a glorious walk,' she returned, 'and I love to look at the sea.'

'It can very rough in winter.' They were walking round the vicarage garden on their way to pick rhubarb for Matty. He said stiffly, 'I hope we shall see more of each other. Are you free at weekends?'

'A day and a half. This is my annual holiday. I'm very lucky to have one; I've only been with Sir Peter and Lady Hensen for three months or so.'

'I'm going back to college next week. When I'm on holiday again, perhaps we could spend a day together.'

'That would be nice. Thank you. Will you be ordained soon?'

'Not for another eighteen months.' He bent to pull the rhubarb. 'There are some charming villages in this part of Essex; we might see something of them?'

'I'd like that very much.' She took some of the rhubarb from him and they went back to the house presently. Then she bade the vicar and his wife goodbye and walked Matty back to her cottage.

'A nice young man, David,' observed Matty as they made their leisurely way through the village.

'Yes. I expect he'll make a good clergyman.' Henrietta added, 'He suggested that when he was on holiday again and I had a free day we might go and look at some of the villages round here. I thought that was very kind of him.'

'Very,' agreed Matty, and stored that little piece of news away to tell Mr Adam when he came. Playing Cupid at my age, she told herself, with an inward chuckle; I ought to know better!

On Saturday morning Henrietta took extra pains with her appearance. She washed her hair, searched—in vain—for spots on her face, applied cream and powder and lipstick and got into the green dress and went down to breakfast. Matty offered her a boiled egg and toast and remarked, 'That's a pretty dress, dearie. A pity that you screw up your hair in that French pleat—don't you ever let it hang loose with a ribbon?'

'Well, no, Matty. We always had to plait our hair at the children's home and I've worn it like this since then; it seemed more—more businesslike.'

'You may be right, but it's a nice head of hair, all the same.'

Henrietta helped with the washing-up then skipped upstairs to make the beds and tidy the bedrooms and bathroom while Matty busied herself in the kitchen— 'For Mr Adam will be wanting his coffee when he comes.'

Come he did, accompanied by the faithful Watson and unloading a box from the boot. He kissed Matty, carried the box into the kitchen, put it on the table and bent to kiss Henrietta too, standing there pouring the coffee.

He stood back and studied her. 'You've got colour in your cheeks at last, and you're nicely plump.'

Her pink cheeks weren't entirely due to the fresh air and sunshine. 'I've had the most marvellous holiday.' Her eyes shone; she looked almost pretty.

'You haven't been lonely?'

'Not for one moment. Matty knows everyone, doesn't she? We've visited so many people and I've been down to the boat yard and we went to the vicarage for tea.'

Mr Ross-Pitt allowed himself an inward chuckle at such unsophisticated pleasures. 'Was David at home? He's at training college...'

'Yes, he showed me the garden. When he comes on holiday again, he said that he would take me to see some of the villages around here—that is, if I'm free to go.'

'Did he?' Mr Ross-Pitt was conscious of a sharp prick of annoyance. His voice was cold and she looked at him in surprise. Matty came in then, and he was instantly his old placid self so that she supposed that she had fancied it.

Since she was to go back with him after their lunch, she said that she would go upstairs and finish her packing. It would give Matty a chance to talk to him. It took less than five minutes to stuff everything into her bag, so she sat down on her bed and looked out of the window and wished she could stay for ever.

She had walked down through the marshes on the previous evening to say her goodbye to the sea; she had done the rounds in the village, wishing everyone goodbye and she had got up very early that morning, stripped her bed and started the washing machine, so that by the time Matty had come down for breakfast the sheets and the bedlinen were already drying on the old-fashioned clothes line in the back garden.

She had vacuumed and dusted her room too, but it worried her that Matty would have extra housework after she had gone—ironing, and all the small chores which were inevitable with visitors.

She glanced at her watch—a necessity that she had had to buy for herself—and decided to stay upstairs for another ten minutes or so—Matty would have a lot to talk about…

Matty had a great deal to say. Adam listened patiently to a blow-by-blow account of the week's activities. 'Such a dear child,' said Matty, 'and very well able to look after herself too. Makes friends wherever she goes, she does. That David up at the vicarage was fair taken with her. Going to take her out for the day when they can fix it up.' Matty cast her listener a sly glance. 'She could do worse, and so could he.'

'Ah,' said Mr Ross-Pitt mildly. 'Love's young dream.'

Matty tut-tutted. 'That I wouldn't know. But if I know Henrietta she's not marrying a man she doesn't love; she'd rather stay single.'

'How do you know that, Matty?'

'I feel it in my bones. And more's the pity, for I doubt she gets much chance to meet the right man, and even if she does who's to know if he'll feel the same?'

'Well, let us hope that things turn out well for her. I'm in your debt, Matty, for taking such good care of her.'

'Bless you, Mr Adam, I've enjoyed every minute of it. She's more than welcome to come whenever she can. And I've told her that.'

There was a short silence. 'And what about you, Mr Adam, if I might be so bold? I did hear from Mrs Dale that you was thinking of matrimony…?' She paused to glance at his face; there was no expression on it—a bad sign—but she went on. 'A Miss Stone, she told me— very smart and handsome.'

'Indeed, Miss Stone is both smart and handsome; she caused quite a sensation when she came to stay with her mother. Mrs Stone knew my mother, you know, years ago, but they occasionally correspond. Which reminds me, Mother is coming down to see you very shortly.

She'll be staying with me for a few days; I'll bring her over.'

'That'll be a real pleasure, Mr Adam.' He hadn't answered any of her questions, Matty reflected, and wondered why. Perhaps he didn't know the answers himself.

When Henrietta came down Mr Ross-Pitt got to his feet. 'I'll take Watson for a quick run while you get lunch,' he suggested. 'I'd like to leave around two o'clock; I'm due back in town this evening.'

The same thought passed through Matty's and Henrietta's heads—Deirdre Stone—but they agreed cheerfully and rather loudly, promised to have everything on the table by the time he got back and bustled around with unnecessary business.

Henrietta had hoped that he would ask her to go with him; lunch was almost ready, there was nothing to do except set the table, for Matty liked to do the cooking, but she hid her disappointment and talked about her holiday, agreeing to Matty's plans that she should come again whenever she could.

'I don't expect you to come every week,' said Matty. 'It's an awkward journey; besides, you've shopping and things to do, but just now and again...'

'Oh, Matty, of course I'll come, and the journey isn't all that awkward. I looked up the buses before Mr Ross-Pitt offered me a lift, and I can come for the day quite easily...'

'You do that, dearie.' Matty had her back to her, bending over a saucepan. 'And if ever you should want a place to go you come here to old Matty.'

Henrietta put down the napkin she was holding, the better to hug the old lady. 'You cannot imagine...' she began, and then tried again. 'Matty, it's like having a family—someone there—I can't explain...'

'No need, for I know just what you mean. Here's Mr Adam back; get the pie from the oven, will you, dear?'

The talk over their meal was cheerful and easy; Mr Ross-Pitt appeared to be in the best of spirits, and Henrietta thought of the journey back with happy excitement—just to sit with him and listen to him talking, never mind what it was about; just the sound of his friendly voice...

Once in the car, waved away by a rather tearful Matty, he showed no signs of wishing to talk, and when she ventured a casual reference to her holiday he answered her with such a casual interest that she held her tongue, supposing his thoughts to be only of Deirdre.

It was a pity that there were some thoughts which were never uttered.

Mr Ross-Pitt supposed with unwonted annoyance that she was thinking about David, so Henrietta sat, bemused by love, not uttering a word while he, in love but as yet unaware of the fact, reminded himself that Henrietta was now with her feet on solid ground—a pleasant job she liked and a worthy young man already interested in her. There was absolutely no reason why he should concern himself with her any more.

He said suddenly, 'You're very quiet—sorry to leave Tollesbury?'

'Yes, indeed I am. It was a marvellous week, and thank you for giving me a lift, Mr Ross-Pitt.'

'There's quite a good bus service to Braintree, then on to Maldon, then the local bus. No reason why you shouldn't spend your free days there.'

In other words, thought Henrietta unhappily, I need not expect another lift. Of course, Deirdre wouldn't like it; it was difficult to imagine Adam giving way to someone else's wishes, but if he was in love with her... There was no way of finding that out; he wasn't a man to wear his heart on his sleeve.

At the lodge she thanked him again in a quiet little voice, patted Watson, and then on an impulse she instantly regretted said, 'I hope you will be very happy, Mr Ross-Pitt.'

He opened his eyes wide at that and she saw their brilliant blue, so often half-hidden by heavy lids. 'Why do you say that?' he demanded.

'Well, you changed my life for me, you know. You have been kind and generous and patient; you so deserve to be happy—and—and I'd like that.'

He said, 'Thank you, Henrietta,' and then got back into his car and drove away.

Mrs Pettifer, peeping from the lodge window, frowned at the sight of Henrietta's face. Mr Ross-Pitt should leave the girl alone. It was apparent to her that Henrietta was head over heels in love with him and, give him his due, he had no idea of it. Henrietta was to him someone he had befriended as he would have befriended a lost puppy or kitten. Oh, well, if the kitchen gossip was anything to go by, that Miss Stone had him hooked.

She went to open the door. Men—even the nicest men—were blind about some things. 'Had a good holiday?' she asked Henrietta cheerfully. 'You look marvellous.'

She led the way indoors, talking all the time to give Henrietta time to assume her usual manner.

'Lovely, Mrs Pettifer. Matty was so kind and I met so many people…'

'One or two of your own age, I hope.'

'Oh, yes. We had tea at the vicarage and the vicar's son was on holiday; he was very kind. When are Sir Peter and Lady Hensen coming home?'

'In a week's time, and before then you and I have a great deal of work to do. There are some old paintings up in the attics that Lady Hensen wants brought down and hung, and there are several pairs of curtains we are to clean and mend and hang in place of those in the big hall. Let's pray for fine, warm weather, then we can take them out onto the lawn; otherwise we must use the ball-room floor.'

That evening, before she went to bed, Henrietta wrote a letter to Matty. Thanking her hadn't been enough, even when she had accompanied her thanks with a box of the chocolates that Matty loved. Besides, the old lady looked eagerly for the postman each morning—letters, she had told Henrietta, were almost as good as a visit.

So she wrote about the curtains and pictures and how pleased Dickens and Ollie were to see her and how charming the country had looked on their drive back. She didn't mention Mr Ross-Pitt. Even thinking about him hurt.

As for Adam, he went home, took Watson for a long walk and shut himself in his study until Mrs Patch came in with a tray of tea.

'Going back tonight, sir?' she wanted to know.

'No, no, I'll go early tomorrow morning, Mrs Patch.' When she had gone he wondered why he had told Henrietta that he had to be back in town that evening. He had done it on an impulse because, he admitted honestly, he was annoyed about David. Although why he should mind about Henrietta making friends with suitable young men quite escaped him. She was a trouble-some girl who for some reason was constantly on his mind.

When Deirdre phoned him later that evening he was unusually terse. He hadn't a free moment during the week, he told her when she suggested that they might dine together one evening, and he put down the phone with relief. He had no wish to see her; indeed, it was only good manners which forced him to speak to her when they met occasionally at a mutual friend's house. She had made it plain that she would like to marry him, and one day he would have to make it clear that he never had any intention of asking her.

Henrietta had little time to think about her holiday or Mr Ross-Pitt. There was a great deal to do before the Hensens returned.

The curtains proved to be in a sorry state—the brocade had worn thin in places, dust had eaten into them and mice had nibbled at their heavy fringes. Luckily it was the fine weather that Mrs Pettifer had hoped for; the lawns were smooth and dry and they could be spread out each day while the pair of them brushed and cleaned and mended with exquisitely small stitches and, since time was of the essence, they went back each evening after their suppers and climbed to the attics to select the paintings that Lady Hensen wanted.

The men carried them down to one of the small rooms leading from the kitchen where they cleaned the frames carefully. There would have to be a professional picture restorer to examine them, said Mrs Pettifer as Henrietta examined the various ancestors, their painted features dim with neglect.

The Hensens returned, the house and grounds were reopened and the days became even busier. Henrietta didn't mind; she didn't want time to hang around heavy on her hands, for then she might lose herself in daydreams about Mr Ross-Pitt and that would never do.

She had had a letter from David in which he said that

he hoped to see her again, and it was tempting to en-
courage him in that hope. After all, since Mr Ross-Pitt
was out of reach, the sooner she forgot about him and
made the best of what life had to offer, the better. Perhaps life was offering her David.

She only thought this during the daylight hours, when
her head was filled with good sense and not romantic
notions. It was at night that she knew that she could
never do that. It would be unfair to David and, besides,
no one could take Adam's place in her heart.

'I shall be an old maid,' Henrietta told Dickens, curled
up on her feet with Ollie snuggled up against his portly
frame.

So she wrote a nice letter back to David telling him
that for the next few weeks she would be extra busy.
'So I expect I'll spend my free day each week recovering
from the hordes of visitors who come each day.' She did
add that later on she hoped to visit Matty again.

It was a week later that she decided to visit Mrs Tibbs
on her free Saturday. She would have a quiet morning
pottering in the lodge, doing a little gardening while
Dickens and Ollie sunned themselves, make herself a
sandwich and then walk to Mrs Tibbs and have her tea
there.

It was a fine day; she did her chores, ate her sandwiches, attended to the cats' wants, got into the floral
dress and walked down to the village, through the lane
and across the fields to Mrs Tibbs' cottage. It was too
early for tea so she walked on for a while, not hurrying
in the sun's warmth and presently she turned back, intent
on tea.

Mrs Tibbs' door was closed, which seemed strange on
a Saturday afternoon when she was almost certain to

have customers. Henrietta knocked and, getting no answer, knocked again.

The cottage stood apart from the others along the lane and she looked around her, wondering what to do. It would be silly to make a fuss just because she couldn't get an answer, and the elderly couple who lived in the first cottage round the bend in the lane kept themselves to themselves, so Mrs Tibbs had told her.

Henrietta trod round the side of the cottage, not wishing to be nosy, but egged on by a feeling that there was something wrong.

The back door was shut but not locked. She knocked again and stood on tiptoe to see inside the kitchen. Mrs Tibbs was on the floor; Henrietta could see only her legs, since her view was restricted, but it was sufficient for her to open the door smartly and go in.

There was a kettle boiling dry on the elderly gas stove and the smell of something burning in the oven. Henrietta turned off the taps and got on her knees by Mrs Tibbs, who was unconscious and a nasty colour—due, no doubt, to the large lump bleeding sluggishly on one side of her head.

Henrietta was no nurse but she had plenty of good sense. She felt for Mrs Tibbs' pulse and found it easily, fetched a cushion from the front room and lifted her head onto it and spoke her name. Mrs Tibbs didn't answer, nor did she respond when Henrietta tried to get her to swallow water.

There was no telephone. Mrs Tibbs had told her once that she would have liked to have had one but her husband thought it would cost too much. 'We ought to have one,' she had added, 'for there's not one along the lane. The nearest one is Mr Ross-Pitt's, and he is all of ten minutes' walk.'

Ten minutes' walk was five minutes' running. Henrietta found pencil and paper and wrote on it 'Don't move, I've gone for help' and propped the message up where Mrs Tibbs would see it if she came round. She laid an old rug lying over the back of a chair over Mrs Tibbs and went out, closing the door behind her.

She ran as fast as she could, urged on by the fact that Mrs Tibbs might be seriously hurt and ought not to be left. She was almost at the wall of Mr Ross-Pitt's house when she saw him watching her from the garden. She had no breath left to shout, but waved her arms in what she hoped was an urgent manner.

The wall was of mellow old bricks, and breast-high to a tall man. Mr Ross-Pitt vaulted over it with the agility of a much younger man and brought her headlong flight to a stop by opening his arms and clasping her to his vast chest.

'It's you,' gasped Henrietta. 'Good. Mrs Tibbs—I went there for tea and she's lying on the kitchen floor and her head's bleeding and she's unconscious—I left a note—'

'Very sensible of you.' He spoke in a calm, soothing voice. 'Come with me; I'll get the car—it will be quicker.'

He wasn't a man to waste time on words; he put a hand on her shoulder and urged her forward along the lane, opened a door in the wall and sat her down on a rustic seat. 'Get your breath,' he advised, 'while I get the car.'

The garage, a roomy affair converted from an old stables, was tucked away behind the shrubbery. Within a minute he had swept the big car round the side of the house, got out, opened her door and ushered her in. He disappeared into the house then, to return with his case and Watson as he said something to Mrs Patch, trotting

behind him. It seemed to take an age to Henrietta before
he got in beside her.

The road curved away from the village after a hundred
yards or so, and he turned into the lane which would
lead them to Mrs Tibbs' cottage.

'Tell me exactly how you found her and what you
did.'

She told him, and he said, 'Good girl,' and didn't
speak again until they drew up outside the cottage.

Mrs Tibbs, naturally enough, was lying exactly as
Henrietta had left her. Mr Ross-Pitt squatted down be-
side her, spared a fleeting moment to chuckle at
Henrietta's note and bent to examine his patient. Hen-
rietta and Watson stood and watched him while he felt
Mrs Tibb's head and then the rest of her.

'No bones broken,' he observed. 'A nasty crack on
the head, though. Concussed—she'll need hospital… Get
me a basin with water and a clean towel, will you?'

He showed no sign of impatience as she hunted round,
coming back presently with what he required. When he
had cleaned the wound and dressed it he said, 'Stay here,
will you? I'm going to phone from the car.' To Watson
he said, 'Stay.'

Henrietta was grateful for the faithful Watson's company; Mrs Tibbs looked very ill, and supposing she came
to and tried to get up? I shall shout for help, decided
Henrietta, common sense coming to the fore.

Mr Ross-Pitt came back. 'Henrietta, will you lay one
of the rugs over the back seat and open the door? I'm
going to drive Mrs Tibbs to Saffron Walden. If we wait
for an ambulance it may do more harm than taking her
in the car. I've warned them and they'll be waiting for
us. You and Watson will sit in front with me.' He
handed her his bag. 'Hang on to that.'

Watson took up a lot of room, but she found his doggy

warmth reassuring as she got into the car and waited
while Mr Ross-Pitt went back to shut the kitchen door.
When he came back he asked, 'Do you know where Mr
Tibbs is?'

'When I have come here before on a Saturday afternoon he has been watching the football match in the
village.'

Mr Ross-Pitt picked up the phone, dialled a number
and handed it to her. 'Mrs Patch will be on the other
end. Ask her to go to the pub and get someone to find
Mr Tibbs and see that he goes to the hospital in Saffron
Walden. He must be told that his wife has had an accident and needs to be examined.'

He was driving fast as he spoke. She repeated the
message, listened to Mrs Patch briskly acknowledging
it, and put the phone back. There didn't seem to be much
point in saying anything. Saffron Walden wasn't far, and
a good thing too, she reflected, watching Mr Ross-Pitt's
large foot on the accelerator.

There was no delay at the hospital; Mrs Tibbs was
wheeled away and Mr Ross-Pitt went with her. Henrietta
and Watson sat side by side in the car in a close prox-
imity which was comforting for them both.

'He won't be long,' said Henrietta, and indulged in a
little daydreaming; he would come out of the hospital
and smile at her lovingly and tell her that she had been
wonderful and he couldn't live without her. She became
so immersed in it that she didn't notice a car draw up
and a man hurry into the hospital—Mr Tibbs, looking
pale with anxiety. She was just waiting for Mr Ross-Pitt
to return.

It was all of half an hour before he did and, if only
she had known it, he stopped at the entrance to look at
her, squashed up with Watson, her rapt gaze on nothing
in particular, dreaming her daydream. Mr Ross-Pitt was

astonished to feel his heart give a decided lurch at the sight of her.

She wasn't looking her best; her hair was coming down, for she had shed hairpins as she'd run, and her face lacked powder and lipstick. She looked hot and tired and surprisingly happy. He thought that he had never seen anyone quite as beautiful, so absolutely necessary to his happiness. It wasn't the first time he had fallen in love, but he knew that this was the last. It would never do to rush her, though...

He got into the car and she turned to smile at him and wondered why he looked so remote.

'Will Mrs Tibbs be all right?'

'Yes. I think so. A hairline fracture and concussion. They'll keep her in hospital for a few days to see how things go. Mr Tibbs got here. You saw him?'

'Me? No, I didn't notice.'

'Well, we'll go back. You must be wanting your tea.' He sounded polite—the politeness of someone who was showing good manners when they were doing something they didn't want to do. 'I'm sure Mrs Patch will have it ready.'

'Please don't trouble—'

'It's the least I can do.' He sounded angry. She longed to have tea with him in his home, but not if he was going to treat her like an unwelcome guest.

She said in a matter-of-fact voice, 'If you don't mind, I'd rather go back to the lodge.'

'Why should I mind?' asked Mr Ross-Pitt savagely, swept away by such a gust of love that he could hardly keep his hands off her. Indeed, if he hadn't been driving that was what would have happened. As it was, they parted at the lodge gate, the air so frigid between them that a knife couldn't have cut through it.

CHAPTER EIGHT

MRS PETTIFER, coming into the lodge half an hour later, was surprised to find Henrietta in the garden with Dickens and Ollie.

'You're back home early,' she observed, and then, catching sight of Henrietta's downcast face, went on hurriedly, 'What a nice surprise for me—and you've got our supper ready too. Did you have tea with Mrs Tibbs?'

She bustled around the little room, taking care not to look at Henrietta, who had come in from the garden.

'Well, I went to see her, but she'd had an accident; she was on the floor with a cut head, unconscious. I—I ran back over the fields for help and Mr Ross-Pitt saw me from his garden and he came and saw to her and took her to hospital.'

'You must have had a busy time, and not very pleasant either. How lucky that you went to see Mrs Tibbs. Poor woman. Of course, her husband would have been down at the football pitch.'

'Yes, but Mr Ross-Pitt phoned Mrs Patch to get someone to tell him. He got to the hospital soon after us.'

'Mr Ross-Pitt must have been glad of your help...'

'I didn't do anything; Watson and I waited in the car while he went into the hospital with Mrs Tibbs.'

'You had your tea at his house, I expect?' Mrs Pettifer put the question casually.

'No,' said Henrietta quietly. 'I preferred not to. Mr Ross-Pitt brought me back here.'

'Just as well,' said Mrs Pettifer briskly. 'I dare say he'll be off this evening. He's much in demand, you know. Wealthy bachelors always are.'

* * *

Adam wasn't going anywhere; he refused the tea that Mrs Patch offered him and went into the garden, where he spent an hour digging out the roots of a dead tree. It was hard work even for a man of his strength, but it cleared his mind so that presently he went indoors, showered and changed, took Watson for his walk and came back for his dinner, outwardly the calm man whom everyone knew as such.

Afterwards, sitting by the open door to the garden, he allowed his thoughts to roam. He supposed with hindsight that he had been in love with Henrietta for quite some time, probably since he had first seen her, but he had been unwilling to admit it even though she had never been far from his thoughts.

He stirred Watson, lying at his feet, with a gentle toe. 'I am afraid that she looks upon me as someone from another world. Oh, she is grateful for any help that I have offered her, and she is friendly in a guarded fashion, but I am too old for her, leading a life so different from hers. I dare say that in time she will fall in love with a young man of her own age—David, perhaps. She would make a splendid curate's wife—matter-of-fact, kind and gentle, with a sound knowledge of how the other half live. Nevertheless, my dear Watson, despite the drawbacks I want her for my wife.'

Watson wagged his tail. 'Good—you approve,' said Mr Ross-Pitt.

Henrietta hadn't expected to see Mr Ross-Pitt in church the next morning; she had made up her mind that he had gone back to London on the previous evening, most likely to spend it with the hateful Deirdre.

The sight of his broad back in one of the pews in front caused all godly thoughts to fly out of her head. It wouldn't be possible to leave before the service was over; if she did half the village would want to know why

when next she saw any of them. Besides, one of the
sidesmen had closed the door, and it made a good deal
of noise when it was opened.

She sang and prayed and sang again, listened with
tremendous concentration to the sermon and, the moment the vicar and choir had gone into the vestry,
whipped through the door before anyone else. No one
would have noticed.

Mr Ross-Pitt had. He made his leisurely way out of
the church, had a few words with the vicar, accepted an
invitation to have drinks with the Hensens and watched
Henrietta's small person hurrying away in the distance.

The Hensens had come in their car and offered him a
lift, but he pleaded the need for exercise and with the
promise that he would see them shortly at the manor set
off across the churchyard.

Henrietta came to the door when he knocked, but not
before she had peeped through the window first to see
who was there. She had had the time to school her features into a look of polite enquiry when she opened the
door, causing Adam to say something quite different
from what he had intended.

His good morning to Henrietta was coolly friendly.
'You may like to know that Mrs Tibbs has recovered
consciousness, but she is to stay in hospital for the next
week or ten days to make certain that there is no worse
damage. She is in the woman's surgical ward; you may
like to send her a card.'

'Thank you for telling me. I'll certainly do that, and
when she's home again I'll go and see her. The evenings
are so light now I could go after I've finished work.'

Adam frowned. 'Don't do that. I know this isn't the
East End of London, but we do occasionally get the odd
stranger roaming around. If you wish to do so, kindly
let me know and I'll drive you over one evening.'

'How kind,' said Henrietta. She would do no such

thing, and what nonsense about going out alone in the evenings. She might love him with all her heart, but that didn't mean to say that he could tell her what she could or could not do.

Ollie darted out and she stooped to pick him up, which filled in the silence between them, and after a moment Mr Ross-Pitt said, 'Well, I must get on—I'm on my way to the manor.' His goodbye was pleasant but a trifle frosty.

As he continued it struck him that Henrietta's reply to his request that she shouldn't go to Mrs Tibbs' alone had been very meek. He made a mental note to keep an eye on her. At the same time they must get back onto their friendly footing…

A patient man, but used to getting what he wanted even if he had to wait for it, Adam pictured a delightful future with Henrietta.

Mrs Pettifer bought a card for Henrietta to send on Monday—roses and forget-me-nots and a puppy in a basket; the choice at the village shop wasn't very wide. Henrietta wrote that as soon as Mrs Tibbs was back home she would come and see her. She told Mrs Pettifer this and that lady frowned. 'I'm not sure that it's a good idea to roam around in the evenings. Mrs Tibbs is a bit isolated.'

'Perhaps her husband would see me back,' hazarded Henrietta.

'That's true. You must be back, though, before it's quite dark. All the same, I'm not happy about you going. You'd better wait until your free day.'

Henrietta said, 'Yes, Mrs. Pettifer,' in the same meek voice that she had used to Adam, only Mrs Pettifer, not being in love, wasn't suspicious.

Henrietta had a note from Mrs Tibbs at the end of the week; she would be going home on the following

Wednesday and hoped that Henrietta would be able to go and see her. She was up and about and her husband would be there to help look after her.

Henrietta said nothing to Mrs Pettifer; Mr Tibbs would be there to see her at least part of the way back; she could come to no harm.

On the following Friday evening fate played into her hand; Mrs Pettifer went back to the house to fetch the notes that Lady Hensen had made concerning the bank holiday opening, and while she was gone Henrietta wrote a note saying where she was, and then armed with some flowers from the garden, set off for Mrs Tibbs' cottage.

It was a warm, light evening, but most of the village were indoors having their late tea and watching television.

With a wary eye she hurried past Adam's garden, but there was no sign of anyone at home; she crossed the fields and presently tapped on the cottage door. Told to come in, she opened it and found Mrs Tibbs sitting in her small front room alone.

'Miss Henrietta, am I glad to see you! Bless you for coming. Hubby's here, but he's in bed; been doing overtime, he has. I was just sitting here wishing I had someone to talk to...'

Henrietta made tea, found a packet of biscuits and put them on the small table between them. She could see that Mrs Tibbs was longing to talk, and talk she did! A blow-by-blow account of her stay in hospital and how she'd come to fall down in the first place.

'Tripped up, I did, on a bit of torn lino, and knocked myself out on that dresser. Thankful I am that you came along when you did.' She beamed at Henrietta. 'And lovely to have a bit of company. Busy up at the manor, are you?'

* * *

Henrietta glanced at her watch—the evening had flown; it was already dusk. She washed up the mugs and put the flowers in a vase, promised that she would come again, and let herself out into the lane. She wished then that she had brought a torch.

The lane, overhung with trees and high hedges, was gloomy; she was glad when she had reached the fields. She could still see the path quite clearly, and there were lights in the village ahead of her—a reassuring sight.

She walked on happily enough, unaware of the man following her furtively, making no sound until suddenly he laughed.

By the time she heard him he was close. She took to her heels and ran, giving a nice healthy scream while she still had the breath. There was still some way to go; she ran on, terrified that she would fall.

Mr Ross-Pitt, sitting by his open window, heard the scream. He was out of the window, through the gate and running almost before it was over, the faithful Watson lumbering along at his heels. One scream sounded very like another, but he knew that it was Henrietta, and what she was doing roaming around on her own was something he would find out later.

He was halfway across the field by now and the man had seen him; he paused, turned, and then ran off as Henrietta hurtled into Mr Ross-Pitt's arms. She gave a great, gasping breath. 'Oh, it's you,' she wailed.

'Indeed it is I. What the devil are you doing out here alone, Henrietta? I told you—'

She took no notice of this. 'It's always you.' She sounded cross. She disentangled herself from his hold and stood, shivering a little, staring at him. 'I never do anything right.' She looked over her shoulder.

'You're a silly girl. He's gone.' He turned her smartly round and marched her back to his garden door. She hung back, but he gave her a gentle shove. 'In you go; you'll have a drink before I take you back to the lodge.'

'I don't want—' began Henrietta.

'Doctor's orders,' he told her in a no-nonsense voice.

She was sat down in his drawing room, fussed over gently by Mrs Patch, comforted by Watson's cold nose and given a glass of brandy to drink by Mr Ross-Pitt. She sipped it gingerly, never having drunk it before, and felt the warm glow from it—which was a good thing, she thought, for there was no warmth in Mr Ross-Pitt's manner, only an impersonal concern for her. Just like a doctor—but then he was a medical man, thought Henrietta, and wished herself anywhere but where she was.

Mr Ross-Pitt left her with Mrs Patch and went to his study where he phoned the lodge. Before he could speak Mrs Pettifer said urgently, 'Henrietta went to Mrs Tibbs—I told her not to—and she's not back—'

'I have her here. Some tramp or other chased her across the fields. I've given her a stiff brandy and she'd better go straight to bed. Extremely silly of her.'

'Oh, dear. Don't be too hard on her; she was being kind to Mrs Tibbs.'

'I should like to wring her neck,' said Mr Ross-Pitt, and rang off.

Ten minutes later he drove Henrietta home. She sat silently beside him, very dishevelled, her hair loosened from its pins, and smelling strongly of brandy. Although she had nothing to say she hiccoughed from time to time, due to the brandy.

Adam felt a great wave of tenderness sweep over him, coupled with a strong wish to laugh. Why, in heaven's name, he reflected, had he chosen to fall in love with Henrietta? It seemed to him that the only times that they saw each other were when she needed his help. The sooner we marry, he decided silently, the sooner I'll have peace of mind.

Mrs Pettifer was waiting at the lodge door. She said cheerfully, 'Come on in, dear, and you too, Mr Ross-Pitt, if you'd care to.' She smiled a little. 'I've just made a great pot of tea.'

He opened the car door and gave Henrietta a hand; the brandy was having its effect. 'There's nothing I'd like better, but I have a great deal of work to finish. Henrietta is none the worse; a cup of tea is just what she could do with before bed.'

He handed her over and she put up a hand to her untidy head. 'I'm so very sorry.' She was looking up at him with huge eyes in a pale face. 'You're the very last person in the world I would want to vex. I'll do my best to keep out of your way.' The brandy had gone to her head. 'I've been a nuisance ever since I found Ollie, haven't I? I do hope it hasn't upset your love life!'

He didn't allow himself even the smallest of smiles, although his eyes gleamed beneath their lids. He said gravely, 'Oh, but you have, Henrietta,' and, unable to stop himself, bent and kissed her gently on a cheek.

He got into his car then, bade them goodnight and drove himself back through the village.

Mrs Pettifer sat Henrietta down in the sitting room and put a cup of tea into her hands. 'What a blessing that we have a man like Adam Ross-Pitt living in this village. While the rest of us would be standing around wondering what to do he gets on and does it. He's a famous surgeon, you know. In line for a knighthood, I believe—not that he cares tuppence about that. Now, drink your tea and tell me how Mrs Tibbs is; something kept you there later than you intended, didn't it?'

Henrietta explained, getting a bit muddled. 'I didn't like to leave her until she'd finished telling me about the hospital. She was wanting to talk—Mr Tibbs was in bed, you see. She's quite safe; it was just—she was lonely.'

Mrs Pettifer, who knew how lonely a life Henrietta had lived before Mr Ross-Pitt had stumbled upon her, understood that. 'I understand why you wanted to visit her, and I'm sure your visit did her good, but don't go alone again, Henrietta. I'll go and see the vicar tomorrow and see if he can organise something—brief daily visits until she feels herself again, something like that. Now, off to bed with you; Lady Hensen wants us to wash the Coalport dinner service tomorrow and put it on display before the first tourists arrive.'

So Henrietta went to bed, to sleep at once but to wake in the small hours and think about Mr Ross-Pitt. How ungrateful she must have seemed to him; it would serve her right if he never spoke to her again. Upon reflection she thought that that wouldn't be too difficult, since she had promised to keep out of his way in future.

She wondered if he would tell Deirdre all about it when he next saw her. She thought not; he was a kind man and he must have noticed that Deirdre didn't like her. She allowed her thoughts to dwell on his kiss and went to sleep again.

It wasn't difficult to keep out of his way; he was, Mrs Pettifer told her, spending a week in Newcastle, operating and lecturing. 'And I dare say while he's there he'll visit his mother and father.'

This was exactly what Mr Ross-Pitt did do, driving up from Newcastle-upon-Tyne, glad to have the week behind him. The prospect of a few days at his parents' home was pleasant, and the Northumbrian countryside, once he had left the city, was magnificent.

At Morpeth he left the main road, choosing to take the country roads towards the coast. At Alnmouth he drove through the village, with its charming jumble of houses and little shops and the wide sands stretching away into the distance, and turned into the narrow road leading to a hamlet—a handful of houses, a church and a ruined castle at its back.

His parents' home was built of golden stone; a solid Queen Anne front concealed the more ancient part of the house from a visitor coming up the short drive from the road. It was screened at its back by larch trees, and the lawns around it were bordered by flower-beds. He got out of the car and opened the door for Watson, who gave a cheerful bark and rushed to meet the two dogs running out of the house.

His mother was behind them and he went to kiss her. 'You don't mind Watson? He's been rather boxed in during this week.' He smiled down at her. 'Mother, it is so nice to see you again. Is Father home?'

'Yes, my dear, in the library, but he'll be here at any moment; he will have heard the dogs.' She scanned his face. 'You've had a busy week. Well, a few days here will do you all the good in the world. Here's your father.'

The two men shook hands, and presently they went indoors to drink coffee and exchange family news.

Lady Ross-Pitt sat back presently, not saying much, watching the two men, so alike in every way. Adam was tired and there was something worrying him; perhaps he would tell her before he went back to his own home. He ought to marry, she thought, but only if he had found the right girl.

She frowned a little. Deirdre Stone, whom she disliked but tolerated because she was one of her oldest friends' daughter, had phoned her several times wanting to know if they expected Adam to visit them. 'I've been meaning to come north again,' Deirdre had said, 'and thought it would be delightful to see something of you.'

Lady Ross-Pitt had said that she had no idea when

Adam would be coming, and had felt guilty afterwards in case he was in love with the girl.

She broached the subject later; his father had gone to the local railway station to collect Adam's elder sister and her two children, who had come up from Sussex to stay while her husband was away on business. Once they were in the house Lady Ross-Pitt knew that there would be no chance of talking to Adam. She began cautiously. 'Mrs Patch looks after you, dear?'

'Very well—she runs the house like clockwork; fits in with my awkward hours without a single grumble.'

'If you should marry I suppose you would keep her?'

'Most decidedly...'

'Perhaps your wife might not like her. Women are strange creatures,' observed his mother guilelessly. 'When Deirdre Stone came here with her mother she hadn't a good word to say for her. Indeed, she told me that she would get rid of her at once.'

'Mother, dear, let me put your mind at rest. I never have had, nor will I ever have a wish to marry Deirdre.'

'I'm relieved to hear it, Adam. I'm sure you'll find the right girl, only don't leave it too long.'

He got up and walked over to the window; it was a cloudless day and the sea was deceptively smooth and blue. 'I've found her already.' He turned to look at his mother. 'She hasn't found me yet; I'm someone she calls "Mr Ross-Pitt"...'

'Tell me about her.'

So he did, standing there, half-turned away; only when he had finished did he turn and look at his mother.

'She sounds exactly right for you, dear. I look forward to welcoming her.'

Adam smiled. 'You'll love her. I must first rid her of several bees in her bonnet; she has this *idée fixe*, fuelled by kitchen gossip at the manor, that I'm going to marry

Deirdre, and it is perhaps unfortunate that each time she has needed help I have happened to be there.'

'A good thing you were. But, of course, she feels beholden to you.'

'The last thing she said to me was, "I do hope it hasn't upset your love life," as well as assuring me that she would keep out of my way!'

'Adam, has it crossed your mind that she might be in love with you too?'

'In love with me? Certainly not. Why should you think that?' He laughed. 'Why, she avoids me on every possible occasion.'

His mother didn't say anything to that, and a moment later there was a great bustling in the hall and her daughter and grandchildren came running in.

That night, getting ready for bed, she told Adam's father. 'I think she will suit him very well and he's so in love. High time too. He needs a wife and a family—look at him with Billy and Sue; he's splendid with children.'

'She might not have him—'

'Not have him? Good heavens, William, he's a famous man in his profession, he's handsome and he's very well off.'

Sir William chuckled. 'From what you have told me, my dear, she doesn't care for any of these things.'

'Exactly; that's why she will suit him so well.'

Sir William shook his head. 'Women—they're so illogical,' he said, and went away to clean his teeth.

Adam drove back to his home two days later. It was late evening by the time he let himself indoors, but Mrs Patch was still in the kitchen.

'There you are, sir. I've coffee or soup, or perhaps something stronger?'

'Coffee, please.' He took his bag to his study and

leafed through his post, strolling through to the kitchen as he did so. 'I'll have it here, while you have a cup with me and bring me up to date with the local gossip.'

Mrs Patch set the coffee before him with a plate of sandwiches. 'Well, now, nothing much has happened. Been busy up at the manor—more visitors than ever before. I met Henrietta on Saturday morning—looked tired and no wonder, on the go all day and every day. I got her to come in and have a cup of coffee with me; she didn't want to at first but I said as how I was lonely. She wanted to know when you'd be back. Oh, and Miss Stone telephoned, said she'd be coming this way one day this week and hoped to find you in.'

Mrs Patch pursed her lips and looked disapproving. 'I said I'd no idea where you'd be this week. She said something about going up to Northumbria.'

It was impossible to tell what Mr Ross-Pitt thought about this piece of news. He said merely, 'I've a very busy week or so ahead of me. It's likely that I'll have to stay in town overnight. I'll let you know if and when.'

'You had a nice time with your ma and pa?'

'Delightful; Mrs Masham and the children are staying there for a few days. They all send their love. As soon as she can arrange it Mother will be coming down to see you and Matty.'

It was late when he got to bed, and in the morning he left very early; he was operating later that day, but first he had ward rounds, and private patients to see. He thought that he would stay in town for the greater part of the week so that he could be free on Saturday—Henrietta's day off.

He shut her out of his mind then, and concentrated on his work—removing a large tumour from a young man's brain, repairing a shattered skull, performing a craniotomy to excise an abscess wall...

It was late afternoon before he saw his private

patients, and when he returned to hospital to do a ward round, late though it was, it was to be told that there was an urgent admission—a child with an intercranial haem- orrhage.

So he went back to Theatre again and bent once more to his painstaking surgery. It was the early hours of the morning by the time he got to his flat, and Watson, that patient animal, needed to have a walk.

It was a quiet night and the traffic, such as there was, was still frequent on the main roads, but the streets round the flat were quiet enough. Adam strolled along, glad of the exercise, and presently went to bed to sleep soundly. But not before allowing his thoughts to stray to Henrietta. She would be asleep, he thought as he closed his own eyes.

Henrietta knew that he was back home from his parents'; the kitchen staff had known it almost as soon as he'd put his key in the door, and discussed it over breakfast. And the odd-job man, drinking his mug of tea before he started work, told them that he had met the milkman, who had it from Mrs Patch that Mr Ross-Pitt would probably spend the week in London.

'Keep 'im on the go, don't they?' he observed.

Feathers said with his usual dignity, 'He is an ex-ceedingly skilled surgeon and the village is proud of him.'

Henrietta glowed with pride when she heard that. Never mind that she had nothing to do with his life, that he must regard her as a nuisance, forever popping up at awkward moments. Though not any more, she thought; she had promised herself that she would keep out of his way, but there was nothing to stop her loving him and being glad that he was liked and respected.

It was two days later at their midday dinner that someone mentioned that he would be coming home for the weekend.

'For the dinner party, no doubt,' said Cook. 'Lady Hensen said twelve guests, and he's bound to be one of them. She wants lobster vol-au-vents, roast crown of lamb, and *charlotte russe* and savarin trifle to follow.'

Feathers spoke. 'The house and grounds will be closed on Saturday afternoon. There'll be plenty of work for everyone; the guests will be coming early for drinks. You may have your day off as usual, Henrietta, and take over at dinner on Sunday.'

She heaved a sigh of relief; she would go away and only return in time to have her dinner and get ready for the tourists on Sunday.

Matty had written to her some days ago and asked when she was to see her again. She would phone her as soon as she could and ask if she might spend the night... There was an early-morning bus to Braintree; she might have to wait for the next one, but that didn't matter as long as she was away from the village.

Matty was delighted, and early on Saturday morning Henrietta caught the bus to Braintree. She had to wait there for a bus to Maldon as she had thought, and, since it was still early there was no café open. She sat on the station platform patiently, content that she had achieved her purpose.

By the time she got back on Sunday morning the chance of seeing Adam would be slight, for as soon as she had had her dinner she would be kept busy until the early evening with tourists. She wondered what he was doing, and if Miss Stone had come for the weekend too. Surely if they were to be engaged she would have been included in the dinner party?

The bus came at last and she finished that part of her

journey, caught the bus to Tollesbury and was given a warm welcome by Matty.

Over coffee and some of her Madeira cake Matty asked, 'Isn't Mr Adam home? I half expected that he'd drive you over—such an awkward journey.'

'Well, yes, he's home for the weekend, I believe. There's a dinner party at the manor this evening.'

'He'll be going, no doubt. Now tell me what you've been doing, dearie—busy I dare say, with the visitors. Still quite happy, are you?'

The morning passed pleasantly, and after a splendid dinner of meat pie and one of Matty's steamed puddings Henrietta washed the dishes, tidied up, saw her hostess to her bed for her afternoon nap and took herself off for a walk. It was no use going to the boat yard since it was a Saturday afternoon; she took the lane to the marshes and wandered around happily until it was time to return for tea.

Matty was still resting, so Henrietta set the tea-tray, cut the cake and buttered scones and had the kettle boiling by the time the old lady came downstairs.

'Well, now,' said Matty. 'What a treat not to have to get my own tea. You must come more often, Henrietta.'

They played cards after tea—racing demon and sevens and snap—until dusk crept into the little room and Henrietta got up to lay the table for their supper—cold ham and a salad and crusty bread from the baker at Heybridge.

They went to bed soon after. 'Such a pity you can't stay until the evening,' said Matty. 'You don't have to go too early tomorrow?'

'No, I'm lucky. There's the bus from Maldon to Chelmsford at half past ten, and I can get the train from there to Braintree. There's a bus to the village from there; I'll be back in good time for dinner at the manor.'

'It sounds complicated,' said Matty doubtfully.

 Henrietta said that it was all very simple in a reassuring voice, although secretly she wasn't so sure. If she missed the bus she might have to take a taxi—anything as long as she got back in time to be at her post when the first of the tourists arrived…

They were having their breakfast when the doorknocker was thumped and David opened the door. 'May I come in? I've been to church and heard that you were here, Henrietta. Are you staying for a few days?'

 'I'm going back in an hour or so. I only came yesterday, just for the night.'

He had sat down with them at the table and Matty had poured him a cup of coffee. 'More's the pity,' she observed. 'All that way just for a few hours—not but what it hasn't been the best weekend I've had for some time.'

 'May I drive you back, Henrietta?' David asked. 'We won't need to leave until eleven o'clock—do you have to be back by one o'clock?'

 'Half-past-twelve dinner. It's awfully kind of you, David, but I can get the bus and train; they all connect up. It'll spoil your day—'

 'There you are mistaken. I shall enjoy the trip.' He finished his coffee and got up. 'Thanks for the coffee, Matty; I will be here just before eleven.'

 'Well, now, that's very civil of him,' said Matty, peeping at Henrietta. 'Smitten, is he?'

Henrietta looked surprised and then laughed. 'I don't think so, Matty; he's nice, isn't he? And it's very kind of him to offer me a lift.'

She had been gone for an hour or more, sitting beside David in his shabby little car, when Matty answered the phone.

Mr Ross-Pitt, having got home very late on Friday evening, rose early in the morning and went out with

Watson, hoping to see Henrietta. There was no sign of her and presently he went back home for the breakfast that Mrs Patch would have waiting for him.

There was a handful of people waiting for the mid-morning bus but she wasn't among them, nor, when he strolled through the village when the late morning bus was due, was she on that. He went back home and into the garden where he did some rather ferocious gardening. After lunch he would walk up to the lodge and see if she was there...

He was cutting into a splendid Double Gloucester cheese after an excellent lunch when the doorbell jangled. He listened with half an ear as Mrs Patch went to the door. He wasn't expecting anyone, but it was probably a message from the manor, or the gardener come for his wages. It was neither—it was Deirdre, elegantly dressed for the country, not a hair out of place, smiling charmingly.

'Adam—aren't I awful?' She gave a little shrill of laughter. 'But Mother has gone to my brother for the weekend and I was lonely. I got into the car and somehow I find myself here. Do say you don't mind. If I might stay for a few hours? Actually, I threw a few things into an overnight bag, thinking I might beg a bed from Lady Hensen...'

Mr Ross-Pitt masked his cold rage with good manners. 'Come and sit down,' he invited. 'I am afraid you must be disappointed about the Hensens—they're giving a dinner party this evening. Will you have coffee and a sandwich, perhaps?'

'Oh, please.' Girlishness didn't suit her. 'I'm famished but anything will do—an omelette, perhaps, and a salad?'

Mrs Patch, standing by the door, went away, shutting the door behind her so that no one could hear her give

vent to her outraged feelings. 'The sauce of her,' she
told Watson, who had followed her out of the room. He
had never liked Deirdre.

Mr Ross-Pitt, left without support of any kind, made
shift to play the good host, listening to Deirdre's mind-
less chatter while he wondered how soon he could go to
the lodge to see Henrietta, for that was his purpose in
coming home for the whole weekend. He might get a
chance to telephone; besides, Deirdre would have to go
after tea, since he was going up to the manor that evening.

Mrs Patch came in with a tray of sandwiches and fresh
coffee, having conveniently forgotten about the omelette, and Deirdre, picking her way daintily between egg
and cress and cold ham, said laughingly, 'I dare say your
housekeeper feels that she has enough to do without
bothering about poor little me.'

Mr Ross-Pitt considered several answers to this but
uttered none of them. Presently Deirdre went away to
tidy herself in the hall cloakroom, and he went into the
garden once more, with Watson at his heels.

She joined him ten minutes or so later. 'I had such a
good idea,' she told him. 'I have phoned Lady Hensen—
I knew you wouldn't mind—and I asked if she could
squeeze me into the dinner party. I quite see that it's a
bit awkward at the last minute, but she said she would
find another man. So kind of her.'

He turned to look at her. 'Awkward and, I imagine,
extremely inconvenient.'

'Oh, Adam, not really; besides, she knows how close
we are.'

He looked outraged. 'Just what do you mean by that?'

She saw that she had gone too far. 'Just that we have
known each other for a long time, and our mothers being
long-standing friends… I said I'd go up to the manor
about six o'clock; luckily I've a frock with me.' She saw

his lifted eyebrows. 'One never knows,' she added. 'I mean, anything might happen.'

She gave him one of her charming smiles. 'Let's sit here in the garden; I'm longing to hear what you've been doing.'

Even if he had intended to tell her, he wouldn't have had the chance. She embarked on a résumé of her social life. After a while he didn't listen, merely making appropriate noises at intervals while he thought about Henrietta.

It was a relief when Mrs Patch came out with the tea and he could get up to arrange the table for her.

'You spoil that woman,' said Deirdre. 'You pay her to do the work.'

'Mrs Patch is a trusted member of the household and a friend of my family.'

Deirdre poured the tea and handed him a cup. She said softly, 'You need a wife, Adam—we could get on famously together... I would fit into your life.'

He looked at her with such disbelief that she put her teacup down in its saucer and leaned back in her chair. It was absurd, but he actually looked as though he was going to shake her.

He said in a voice so coldly violent that she flinched, 'Let me make myself plain. I would never, under any circumstances, want you for my wife.' He added, 'Nor have I given you any reason to suppose that I would.'

Deirdre got up, shaking with rage. 'I wouldn't marry you if you were the last man on earth,' she spat at him. 'I hope when you do marry that your wife gives you a rotten time of it. I'm going. You can let Lady Hensen know that I've changed my mind. I never want to see you again.'

Good manners, instilled from early childhood, ensured that he saw her to her car and bade her goodbye.

Meeting him in the hall, his housekeeper said, 'Good

riddance to bad rubbish, if you'll pardon the expression, Mr Adam.'

He could hear the relief in Lady Hensen's voice when he phoned. 'Thank heaven, Adam; what a tiresome woman she is. Come early, will you? Peter wants to show you his plans for the new barn.'

The lodge was in darkness as he went through the gates. Henrietta must be away. His face cleared; of course, she would be with Matty. He drove on up to the manor and spent a pleasant evening. Indeed, those present at dinner told each other afterwards that they hadn't seen him so light-hearted for a long time. 'He must be in love,' someone said. 'I do hope so; he's such a dear.'

Tomorrow morning, Mr Ross-Pitt promised himself, he would go to the lodge and see Henrietta. Only, when he got there soon after breakfast there was no one there, just Dickens and Ollie staring at him through the sitting-room window. She must have stayed the night at Matty's; he would phone.

When he did no one answered; Henrietta was sitting in David's car and Matty had gone into the lane to wish her goodbye. When he tried again later it was Matty who answered.

CHAPTER NINE

'HENRIETTA? She's been gone about an hour, Mr Adam. She's been here—came yesterday. Such an awkward journey too, left ever so early to get here.' Matty gave a chuckle. 'Had a bit of luck, though, this morning. David's given her a lift back to the manor. Cut it a bit fine, though.'

Mr Ross-Pitt said in a voice which gave nothing away, 'Splendid. I'm sure you enjoyed her company, Matty. Are you well? Do you need anything?'

He didn't mention Henrietta again, nor did he make any attempt to see her; she would be showing tourists round until the late afternoon and he had no excuse to call at the lodge; besides, Mrs Pettifer would be there.

He spent the rest of the day working in his study, only coming out in order to take Watson for a walk. He was a man of patience; he wanted Henrietta but he might have to wait a long time for her, perhaps lose her; David was a decent young man and her own age. Mr Ross-Pitt, sitting there behind his handsome desk, felt decidedly middle-aged. Not that he had any intention of giving way to despair, rather would he bide his time.

Henrietta got to the lodge with ten minutes to spare, so that her thanks to David were hurried. It had been a pleasant journey and, since she was a person people confided in without realising it, she had soon been the recipient of David's plans for the future.

There was a girl, he'd told her; he had met her at a friend's house. 'She's eighteen,' he had said, 'but she

167

says she'll wait—I've got another eighteen months before I'm ordained... Do you think she would be too young to marry?'

'Heavens, no, especially as you love each other; and what a support she will be to you, David. I mean, you'll grow old together, you'll have all your lives to look forward to. What do her parents think about it?'

'They don't think we should be engaged yet.'

'Why ever not? If I were you I'd buy a ring and put it on her finger.'

He had laughed then. 'Do you know, I believe that I will?' he'd said.

They had parted on excellent terms and she had hurried up to the manor just in time to sit down at the table for the Sunday dinner that Feathers insisted they all attended.

'Had a nice time?' asked Cook, dishing out Yorkshire pudding with a lavish hand.

'Yes, thank you, Cook. Matty is so kind and I went for a long walk.'

Addy gave her a pitying glance. On her own, no doubt. Poor kid—a fat chance she had of getting to know any young men; besides, she didn't make much of an effort to go and look for one. Addy, who had what she called her 'steady', as well as several casual boyfriends, felt sorry for her.

Henrietta, unaware of Addy's concern, ate her dinner, bore her share of the talk, helped clear away the dishes and went to make sure that everything was in readiness for the tourists.

Sunday afternoons were always busy, and over and above that those who came weren't really interested in the lovely furniture and china, and they didn't care a button for the portraits of dead-and-gone Hensens; they came out of curiosity, to stare around the rooms to see how the other half lived and, if possible, peep behind closed doors.

Henrietta, reciting her spiel, pausing hopefully for someone to ask a question—any question to let her know that someone was interested—found it hard to talk to such an unresponsive audience. Now and again there would be someone for whom it was all worthwhile, someone who asked questions about the portraits and knew something about the silver and porcelain, who shared her delight in everything.

Not this afternoon, however. Each group had a number of children, bored with going from room to room, breaking away from restraining hands, crying and shouting. The vicar's wife, roped in to give a helping hand, raised long-suffering eyebrows as their respective parties met and passed in the ballroom.

The last group left at last; the vicar's wife said, 'What a frightful afternoon,' and left too, leaving Henrietta to go from room to room checking that everything was still there and that nothing had been broken or torn. She didn't hurry because as usual she was thinking about Adam, unaware of the contretemps on Saturday.

It was Mrs Pettifer who had begged everyone to say nothing of it to Henrietta, and Feathers had backed her up.

'She owes a great deal to Mr Ross-Pitt and has a real regard for him. She said only a few days ago that she hoped he would be happy with Miss Stone. We don't want her upset, do we?' She'd looked around at the faces raised to hers. 'She's had a poor deal so far, we all know that, and I think she's happy now. Let's keep it that way.'

They had all agreed. It was Lady Hensen who let the cat out of the bag. Passing through the great hall, she stopped to speak to Henrietta, busy arranging the giant epergne just so on the long refectory table.

'Ah, Henrietta, you've had a busy afternoon. You went away for the weekend, Mrs Dale tells me. You had an enjoyable time?'

'Yes, thank you, Lady Hensen.'

'You missed such a stupid fuss on Saturday evening. My dinner party was almost ruined. Miss Stone—I believe you have seen her here?—phoned from Adam's house to say that she was staying there and could I possibly squeeze her in for dinner. Well, I ask you, at a moment's notice; it meant getting another man at the last minute, but I couldn't refuse without being rude...

'And do you know that after I'd spent hours looking for an extra man Adam phoned to say that Deirdre had changed her mind? All that fuss for nothing. He didn't say a word about it when he came and I haven't asked him. He looked extremely pleased with himself, though.'

She broke off to eye Henrietta. 'I should finish here, Henrietta; you're tired out. You need a cup of tea; you're quite pale.'

Lady Hensen went on her cheerful way and Henrietta sat down carefully on one of the chairs lining the panelled walls—an armchair of the French Empire style with Chinese motifs, and priceless. She sat quietly for a few moments. It wasn't any use being silly about it, she told herself; Deirdre Stone was going to marry Adam and that was an end of the matter. It was, after all, what she had expected, wasn't it? So why did she feel bereft? She was no part of his life, just someone whom he had helped when help had been so badly needed. She must wish him well from the bottom of her heart and stop behaving like an emotional idiot.

She got up then, dusted the chair carefully and went to the kitchen where Cook was waiting with a pot of tea.

'You've 'ad a busy afternoon, I can see. Sit down, do,

Henrietta and drink your tea. There's a batch of scones straight from the oven. Help yourself.'

Henrietta managed the tea but not the scones, sitting there at the long table, alone, for teatime for the kitchen was long past. She was drinking her second cup of tea because Cook insisted when Mrs Pettifer came in.

'I know I'm not on duty,' she said, and bit into a scone, 'but I had to come back for my library book; I left it here…' She took a look at Henrietta's face. 'You've had a bad afternoon by the look of you.'

'Not bad at all,' said Henrietta in a bright voice which didn't sound quite like hers. 'Lady Hensen came into the great hall while I was tidying up; she told me about Miss Stone.'

'Ah.' Mrs Pettifer exchanged a quick glance with Cook. 'Yes, a bit of a mystery, so it seems. I dare say we'll hear the right of it one day. Mr Ross-Pitt isn't a man to tell tales, though, and Mrs Patch is very loyal.' She added, 'I'm not going away this evening; I fancy a nice quiet day doing nothing with Dickens and Ollie.'

She was rewarded for her change of plan by Henrietta's grateful look. The child wears her heart on her sleeve, reflected Mrs Pettifer. She plunged into a cheerful account of her long afternoon with friends in Braintree, which gave Henrietta time to pull herself together, and presently they walked back to the lodge, talking about everything under the sun except Mr Ross-Pitt.

Mr Ross-Pitt, back at the hospital on Monday, immersed in his busy daily round, kept his mind firmly on his work, and no one who had reason to be with him would have guessed at his bottled-up frustration and rage.

He operated with his usual calm, thanked the theatre staff when the list was over, drank coffee with his theatre sister and then did a ward round with his registrar and a clutch of medical students, all of whom he treated with a patient courtesy which caused even the dullest of them to give the right answers to his questions.

After that he left the hospital to see his private patients at his rooms. They, he thought privately, were much harder to deal with than his students; the elderly man with Parkinson's disease was relieved to hear that an operation might give him some respite and left after profuse thanks, but the other two patients, told gently that they would need surgery for tumours of the brain, behaved rather differently.

The elder of them, a woman of more than middle age, took refuge in rage and disbelief, both of which he could understand even if it made life for him trying. It was a normal reaction, which he had seen many times, and he used all his skill and kindness to overcome it—something which took time. As for his last patient, a young woman still, she simply did not believe him, and when he had at last convinced her that he must operate she fainted. It was fortunate that she had someone with her— her mother—but it took him some time to soothe his patient sufficiently to arrange for her to enter the hospital she had chosen. It spoke a great deal for the kind of man he was that by the time she left his rooms she had accepted his diagnosis without further fuss.

He went back to the hospital to finish his day, tired now and wanting to be home. And, more than that, he wanted to be home with Henrietta there with him.

It was well past six o'clock by the time he got into the car and started for home; the worst of the rush hour had passed and he made good time. It was a fine evening, and once he had left the city and its suburbs behind he allowed his thoughts to wander. It would have been good sense to have stayed at his flat for the night, he reflected, for he would have to leave early the next morning since he had to operate at one of the big private hospitals at nine o'clock, but he had the admittedly foolish wish to be near Henrietta, even if only for a few hours of the night and with the length of the village between them.

Later, having eaten Mrs Patch's delicious supper, he took Watson for his walk as far as the lodge, to stand like a lovesick youth and look up at the lighted window where his Henrietta was getting ready for bed. He checked a desire to bang on the door and demand to see her and continued on his way, tiring himself and Watson out before reaching his home again.

He was barely out of sight of the lodge when Henrietta put out the light and went to the window to draw back the curtains. She stood for a minute or so looking out at the not quite dark night, her head as usual full of thoughts of Adam. Most certainly, had she gone to the window five minutes earlier and had he given way to his impulse and thumped the knocker, she would have rushed down and opened the door...

Henrietta planned her Saturday very carefully. She had to avoid Mr Ross-Pitt at all costs, so she would spend the day in Saffron Walden and, in order to make sure that she wouldn't meet him in the village, she had prevailed upon the grocer's van driver from that town to give her a lift. He came every so often with groceries that Cook had ordered—groceries which the village shop or even Thaxted were unable to supply—and when most providentially he had called during that week she had seized the opportunity to ask him.

He'd agreed readily enough. 'Though I'm not hanging around if you're not ready by half past nine,' he'd told her.

She spent the day looking at the shops, choosing the clothes she would like to buy if she had the money. True, she had the money now, but the future, for all its promise, could be uncertain, and she had promised herself that

she would never go back to the life she had led before
Mr Ross-Pitt had rescued her. Not only that, she would
have to go once she had saved enough money; to stay
in the village near him wouldn't help her to forget him.
Her plans for the future were vague but inescapable; she
was determined to carry them out.

She had lunch in a small café and took herself off to
look at the timber-framed houses and admire the par-
geting on the brick and flint houses of a slightly later
date. They had worn well during the four hundred years
of their existence.

She visited the church of St. Mary the Virgin too, and
then, still with time on her hands, explored the keep of
the Norman castle. A late tea took her to well after five
o'clock and she caught the evening bus back.

Adam, if he was at home, would be indoors now,
probably getting ready to go to Deirdre or dining out
with some of his friends. She would be safe.

All the same, she got out of the bus cautiously, but
there was no one about; the tourists had long since gone
and the village had settled down to Saturday high tea
and the telly.

She was almost at the lodge when she saw him coming towards her down the drive. If she ran she might get
to the lodge first and go in and shut the door, pretending
that she hadn't seen him, but then he might find that a
strange thing to do. For all she knew he was out for an
evening stroll with Watson. Anyway, it was too late
now; he had reached her.

Mr Ross-Pitt, at the sight of her, had found himself
positively engulfed by strong feelings. No longer the
calm, reserved man, admired for his cool composure in
the face of difficulties, he reached her in a few rapid
strides, caught her in a fierce embrace and kissed her.

Henrietta, taken aback, allowed herself to enjoy his
kiss. Indeed, she had no idea that being kissed was such

utter bliss; the world, as far as she was concerned, didn't exist, nor did the Hensens, or her job or Mrs Pettifer... It was Watson's gentle bark, reminding them that he was there, which brought her back to her senses.

She gave a not very effective push against Adam's vast chest. 'This will not do,' she declared. 'Whatever next? Please go away quickly and forget all about this— this regrettable incident.'

Even in her own ears this sounded pompous, which was probably why he laughed. 'You liked it as much as I did, Henrietta.'

'Yes, I did.' She had disentangled herself by now and stood facing him. 'Indeed I did, but it was quite wrong. I'm sorry it happened and it wasn't very fair of you. I mean, I did tell you that I would keep out of your way and I meant that. I really would rather not see you, and you must know why. I'll always be grateful to you, you know that, but we have to think of other people who might not like—'

He interrupted her in a suddenly cold voice. 'Ah, yes, of course, you have your future to consider, do you not? I don't imagine David is a jealous man, but it wouldn't do to risk that, would it?' He went on pleasantly now, 'My apologies, Henrietta—I shall do my best to ignore you when we next meet.'

He whistled to Watson, who, bored, had walked away, and left her there.

She made no move to go into the lodge. What had he meant about David? If only he had waited a minute and given her time to gather her wits about her she would have asked him. How could David be jealous when he had a girl of his own? Why had Adam kissed her like that when everyone knew that he and Deirdre were going to marry? It was a foregone conclusion in the kitchen.

She did go in finally, to greet Dickens and Ollie, give them their supper and start getting ready a meal for when

Mrs Pettifer came back from the manor. When she had been at the children's home she had frequently been told sternly to count her blessings. She tried to do that now, but not very successfully. For one thing her heart wasn't in it. Her heart, if Adam did but know it, had been given to him.

Henrietta went to church in the morning. She didn't sit in her usual place but chose a pew on the other side of the aisle, prudently sitting between two stout ladies and behind the village policeman, who was over six feet tall and with a massive girth; thus she was sure that Mr Ross-Pitt, even if he bothered to look, would never see her. She was wrong, of course, but he gave no sign that he had, leaving the church in the Hensens' company, to all intents and purposes a man well-pleased with his world.

Henrietta waited until they had paused at the end of the churchyard to speak to old Colonel Blake and his wife and then took herself off at a smart walk, intent on being out of sight as quickly as possible. Adam, listening with seemingly deep interest to the colonel's pithy observations concerning the poor state of the country's politics, watched her go.

He had no intention of going after her—not at the moment; he had every intention of seeing her again and, provided nothing urgent turned up during the next week, he should get home each evening, and if necessary he would bang on the lodge door until she was forced to see him. After all, it wasn't she who had mentioned David; perhaps he had jumped to the wrong conclusion.

Mr Ross-Pitt, so sane and assured in his judgements, was discovering that Henrietta had, as it were, thrown a spanner into them. In that case, who were the people who might not like...like what?

He phoned Matty that evening, and after a suitable

exchange of news asked, 'Matty, has David fallen for Henrietta? He brought her back, didn't he? Came to see her...?'

'Bless you, Mr Adam, whatever gave you such an idea? Why, David's got a girl already, but of course they'll have to wait until he's ordained. He and Henrietta get on well—like brother and sister, you might say.'

She hesitated. 'Mrs Patch gave me a ring this morning, told me all about that Miss Stone. There's a shocking lady for you, and no mistake, setting everyone by the ears. Perhaps I shouldn't be saying that to you, sir?' It sounded like a question.

'Matty, you know very well that you can say what you like to anyone in the family. Miss Stone has lost all interest in me and the family.'

'Your ma will be pleased!' said Matty in a contented voice.

Mr Ross-Pitt rang off. So it wasn't David, which made things easier but not all that much. Perhaps his Henrietta had silly notions in her head about their different ways of life—something he felt sure that he could solve if only he could get her to listen to him.

The first thing that he did when he got to his rooms on Monday morning was to instruct his secretary to make no appointments after four o'clock, and then later, in the hospital, he went over his week's schedule with his registrar, making sure that his evenings as far as possible would be free. Emergencies, of course, would have to be dealt with if they arose; they were unavoidable and part of his life.

It was a great pity that after all his careful planning he should receive an urgent request to fly at once to Washington, where a member of the British Embassy had been struck down with a subdural haemorrhage, and whose wife had insisted upon his services and no one else's. He flew out that same afternoon.

Henrietta heard of it in the kitchen, where they had heard of it from the milkman, who had it on the best authority of Mrs Patch. It meant that she was free to walk to the village without looking round every corner first to make sure that he wasn't there; it also meant that she worried about his safety all day and a good deal of each night. Not only his safety; would he get enough rest? And would there be someone to see that he had proper meals? Iron his shirts? And what about Watson?

Excusing herself from her dinner, which she didn't want anyway, she went along to see Mrs Patch, who came to the door with Watson at her heels.

'Henrietta, come in, my dear. Is something the matter? You're not ill?'

'No, no. I'm fine, Mrs Patch. It's just that I heard from the staff that Mr Ross-Pitt has had to go to America, and I wondered about Watson. I mean, his walks…'

'Bless you for thinking of him. He's that lost without his master. I took him a walk this morning, but I'll have to get someone to take him for his proper run in the evenings. My legs aren't up to it.'

'Would I do, if Mrs Pettifer doesn't mind? I could take him along the drive up to the house and back and he could run loose. Only I'd have to ask first.'

'Would you really? I'm sure I don't know how long Mr Adam will be away, but if things don't go as they ought he might be there for several days—weeks, even.'

She patted Henrietta's arm. 'You must have missed your dinner. Just you come in for a few minutes; I've just put everything ready to make an omelette, and there's a loaf just out of the oven and a glass of milk.'

It was strangely comforting sitting in the kitchen in Adam's house, with Watson beside her and Mrs Patch sitting opposite her at the table. 'It's a shame,' declared

Mrs Patch, offering a dish of apples, 'for he told me that he hoped to come home each evening this week without fail—barring emergencies, that is.'

When appealed to, Mrs Pettifer could see no harm in her taking Watson for his evening walk. 'As long as you stay along the drive and are back in good time for our supper.' She saw Henrietta's face light up and gave a relieved sigh. The girl wasn't looking her best... This would give her an interest for a few days.

It was two days later at dinner that Addy told the table her news. 'I was serving morning coffee,' she told them. 'Old Mrs Porter called, and she always expects coffee and biscuits—well, I heard her telling Lady Hensen that Miss Stone has gone to America. Flew over, sudden-like. Good riddance, I'd say—'

'Curb your tongue, Addy,' said Feathers. 'You're speaking of your betters.'

'If that Miss Stone's better than me, I'm a Dutchman,' said Addy—a remark which prompted Feathers to make a dignified speech encompassing rudeness, respect for elders and betters, and not listening to gossip.

'It wasn't gossip,' protested Addy. 'It was Mrs Porter, and if she's my elder and better how can she gossip?'

In the ensuing arguement, in which almost everyone joined, no one noticed Henrietta's stricken face except Mrs Pettifer, who made no comment. Once dinner was over, though, she sent Henrietta up to the attics to look out a pair of ormulu candlesticks that Lady Hensen had decided would look just right on the serving table in the great hall.

'You have plenty of time before two o'clock, when that coachload of children will be coming from Braintree. As long as you're at the entrance by fifteen minutes before the hour.'

So Henrietta went to the attics and, since the candle-

sticks were easily found, she was able to sit down on a
rather tattered love seat and pull herself together. She
was behaving badly, she told herself. After all, she had
known that Mr Ross-Pitt and Deirdre Stone were going
to marry; what could be more natural than for her to go
with him to the States? She would be there to see that
he had enough rest and his proper meals, although it was
unlikely that she would bother about his shirts.

Henrietta shed a few tears; she would have liked to
have wept buckets, but presently she would have to go
downstairs again and present a welcoming face to the
children, so she blew her nose with resolution, wiped
her eyes and took the candlesticks down to Feathers'
pantry, where she asked him politely if she could leave
them there until she had time to clean them.

Feathers, wishing that Addy could learn a few nice
manners like Henrietta, gave his consent. He said graciously, 'Cook has a pot of tea ready in the kitchen—
why not have a cup? There are still ten minutes before
the gates open.'

Henrietta had the tea, foraged in her shoulder bag for
powder and a comb, and then took her place by Mrs
Pettifer's side as the coach drew up. The children tum-
bled out and Mrs Pettifer murmured, 'Thank heaven the
place is closed to visitors for the afternoon; this lot will
keep us busy!'

They divided the children into batches, each accompanied by a teacher. It was to be an educational tour
followed by tea, and it soon became apparent that being
lectured about a lot of old furniture and pictures was
only to be endured provided that there was tea to follow...

A tiresome afternoon, agreed Mrs Pettifer when they
finally reached the lodge. 'I have never had so many
requests for the lavatory as I have had today.'

'Perhaps they weren't quite old enough to appreciate

things,' said Henrietta. 'I must say some of the older boys behaved badly. I shall have to rub up the silver. I'm sure they would never steal anything, but they did like to finger it.'

Mrs Pettifer yawned. 'A busy day for us tomorrow, then. You see to the silver and I'll clean and mend that cushion cover someone tore. We need eyes at the backs of our heads, don't we?'

The week wore on, and Henrietta lay in bed at night making plans. She would have to go, there was no help for it; to have to live in the same village as Mr Ross-Pitt and Deirdre was too much. But where to and to do what? She was sure that Lady Hensen would give her a good reference, but what as? Domestic? Guide? Jill of all trades?... And master of none. She would have to train for something, but what?

She had money now—not a great deal, but she had learnt the hard way how to live on next to nothing and she could do it again. Only not in London—somewhere in the country, where Dickens and Ollie would be welcome and happy. A mother's help, she decided finally, where she would be kept busy all day and would be too tired to think about Adam.

The weekend came and went, and there was no sign or word of him. She wrote a letter full of cheerful news to Matty, visited Mrs Tibbs and took Watson for his evening walk, and never once, when she went to collect him from Adam's house, did Mrs Patch mention Adam.

Monday again, and another week to get through, thought Henrietta, getting dressed, going downstairs to the kitchen to let Dickens and Ollie out into the garden, putting on the kettle and fetching a saucepan for the eggs.

It's time you pulled yourself together, she told herself; you've no business moaning. Remember what life was

like for you before you came here, before you met
Adam? Count your blessings...!

Mr Ross-Pitt, thousands of miles away, his work brought
to a satisfactory conclusion, packed his bag, checked his
instruments and, in the quiet of his room at the British
Embassy, picked up the phone and glanced at his watch.
It would be mid-afternoon in England; Mrs Pettifer
should be at the manor.

It had been a warm day and there had been more tourists
than usual. Henrietta was glad when she and Mrs Pettifer
had finished and could go down to the lodge.

'I'll make a pot of tea, shall I? And I'll get the supper
when I get back from taking Watson for his walk. It's
been busy, hasn't it?'

'Very. Tea would be lovely. While you're gone I'll
make us a salad—we can have an omelette.' Mrs Pettifer
didn't sound at all tired; indeed, she looked pleased with
herself although she didn't say why.

They drank their tea and Henrietta changed into a skirt
and top and comfortable sandals and went to fetch
Watson.

Mrs Patch greeted her with a beaming face. She
looked, thought Henrietta, just as pleased with herself as
did Mrs Pettifer. Henrietta put the lead on Watson and
walked him up to the drive where she let him loose for
a time before taking him back.

'I'll come tomorrow at about the same time,' she told
Mrs Patch.

'Yes, dear,' that lady said. 'He does love his walks.
I'm afraid his morning trot is short; this weather plays
havoc with my corns.'

She still looked pleased about something, and
Henrietta had a sudden, heart-stopping thought—perhaps
Mr Ross-Pitt was coming home. Bringing Deirdre with

him? No, it couldn't be that; there hadn't been a murmur in the kitchen, and they always knew everything. She went back to her supper and then stayed in the little garden with Mrs Pettifer, idling away an hour or so before bed.

Mrs Pettifer kept her very busy the next morning, and even when she had a spare minute or two there was Mrs Dale wanting her to go and find the gardener and remind him to bring up the flowers for the house, and Cook sending her back to him again to ask for some fresh parsley.

In the afternoon there were the visitors. Not as many as usual, but mostly elderly and well informed, stopping to discuss this or that picture or admire a particularly fine piece of furniture. Mrs Pettifer left her to take the last group round and it was past five o'clock by the time she had ushered them out of the entrance, apparently unhurried, listening to their thanks and comments and longing for a cup of tea.

She turned back to the house at last and found Mrs Pettifer crossing the hall to her.

'Run and have your tea, Henrietta, and then go back to the lodge. I'll go round and take Addy with me. You had more than your fair share this afternoon.' She tapped Henrietta on the arm. 'Do as I say now. I'll be along presently.'

Henrietta drank her tea while Cook told her about her nephew, who had just passed his driving test. 'I'll see 'im on Sunday,' she said happily. 'Bake 'im a cake.' She glanced at Henrietta. 'Run along, ducks—you look fair tuckered.' She frowned over her pastry. 'Working you too 'ard, are we? You've been looking a bit peaky, and no second 'elpings at dinner...'

'I'm fine, and the food's so delicious I don't need second helpings, Cook.' She took her cup and saucer to the scullery. 'It will be nice to sit in the garden for a bit. It was hot in the house today…'

It was still warm. She felt tired, despite her brave words to Cook. When she got to the lodge she would have a shower and change her clothes and do her hair and face. She always presented a neat and pleasant picture as she led tourists round the house, but she felt that she must be looking a fright at the end of this afternoon. Her head ached a little too; she would take the pins out of her hair and just tie it back. She took the key from her shoulder bag and unlocked the door and went into the sitting room.

Mr Ross-Pitt was sitting there, in Mrs Pettifer's chair, with Dickens and Ollie on either side of him and Watson sprawled at his feet. Not Mr Ross-Pitt, thought Henrietta wildly, but Adam, calm and elegant and tired to his bones; her dear Adam… Only he wasn't; he was Deirdre's.

Mr Ross-Pitt got out of the chair, gently spilling Dickens and Ollie onto the floor. He hadn't spoken, but now he came to loom over her.

An awkward situation, reflected Henrietta, supposing that he had come to see Mrs Pettifer about something. She took a deep breath to calm her racing heart. 'You're back from the States,' she said in a polite voice, with only the slightest quaver in it. 'Did you have a nice trip?'

'No,' said Mr Ross-Pitt.

She tried again. 'When did you get back?'

'About three hours ago.'

If only he would talk. 'You must be tired. I expect you would like a cup of tea; I'll put the kettle on.'

'I would not like a cup of tea. I would like you, Henrietta.'

Her eyes and, regrettably, her mouth opened wide. 'Me? Whatever do you mean?' She remembered then.

'Is Deirdre with you? I mean, did she come back with you?'

Mr Ross-Pitt was beginning to enjoy himself. 'You expected her to do so?'

'Well, yes. I mean, if she went with you she must have wanted to come back with you, if you see what I mean.'

'I am doing my best to follow your train of thought, but it is a little difficult since we are at cross purposes.'

Anxious to have the conversation over and done with, and Adam gone so that she might go somewhere dark and quiet and have a good cry, Henrietta took another deep breath. 'The kitchen knew you'd gone to the States; the milkman had it from Mrs Patch, and he told Cook who told us...'

Mr Ross-Pitt put his hands in his pockets and his handsome head a little on one side; he looked the picture of casual ease. Henrietta, on the other hand, was pale and untidy, her hair in wisps, her nose shining—by no means a captivating picture. Mr Ross-Pitt thought she looked adorable. 'Yes?' he murmured encouragingly.

'Then Mrs Porter told Lady Hensen—while they were having coffee and Addy took in the tray and heard what she was saying—that Miss Stone had flown to the States, too—to be with you, of course!'

'Of course! Henrietta, if I tell you that I have no idea where Deirdre Stone is, nor do I wish to know, and that I had no idea until this moment where she had gone, nor do I care, will you believe me?'

She stared up into his face; he didn't look tired any more. She said, 'Yes, of course I believe you.'

'Good. Having disposed of the tiresome woman, let us forget her and allow me to do what I have come to do.'

'What's that?' This was a lovely dream; presently she would wake up.

'Kiss you,' said Mr Ross-Pitt. 'Something I should have done when you first trod all over me.' He took her in his arms and held her tight. 'I shall kiss you until you have just enough breath left to say that you'll marry me.'

For the moment it was impossible to answer that, but presently Henrietta said in a small voice, 'But you haven't asked me...'

He kissed her again, slowly and thoroughly. 'My dear heart, will you marry me, and soon? We have wasted so much of our time. We may have met only by chance, but it is clearly meant that we should meet and love and marry.'

'You never said—if you had told me...'

He kissed her untidy head. 'I shall tell you that I love you every day of our lives.'

'Just once will do!' said Henrietta.

Take 2 bestselling love stories FREE
Plus get a FREE surprise gift!

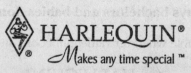

✦ *Harlequin Romance*®

We're proud to announce the "birth" of a brand-new series full of babies, bachelors and happy-ever-afters: ***Daddy Boom***. Meet gorgeous heroes who are about to discover that there's a first time for everything—even fatherhood!

Starting in February 1999 we'll be bringing you one ***Daddy Boom*** title every other month.

February 1999: **BRANNIGAN'S BABY**
by Grace Green

April 1999: **DADDY AND DAUGHTERS**
by Barbara McMahon

We'll also be bringing you deliciously cute ***Daddy Boom*** books by Lucy Gordon, Kate Denton, Leigh Michaels and a special Christmas story from Emma Richmond.

Who says bachelors and babies don't mix?

Available wherever Harlequin books are sold.

HARLEQUIN®
Makes any time special ™

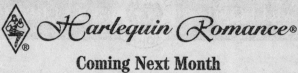

Coming Next Month

#3539 BACHELOR AVAILABLE! Ruth Jean Dale

Cody James was tall, sexy and handsome—he took Emily Kirkwood's breath away. Too bad that Emily hadn't joined the Yellow Rose Matchmakers to find a man but to write a Valentine's story on... well...how to get a man. Only, Cody *was* available...and perhaps what this story needed was a little in-depth research!

Texas Grooms Wanted! *Only cowboys need apply!*

#3540 BOARDROOM PROPOSAL Margaret Way

It's the job of her dreams, but can Eve Copeland believe that she won it fairly and squarely? Her new boss, after all, has a secret he'd go to great lengths to conceal....

#3541 HER HUSBAND-TO-BE Leigh Michaels

Deke Oliver was convinced Danielle was trying to manipulate him into marriage—just because they'd jointly inherited a property...and were forced to live together under the same roof! But Deke wasn't husband material, and Danielle simply *had* to convince him that she wasn't dreaming of wedding bells!

#3542 BRANNIGAN'S BABY Grace Green

When Luke Brannigan asked Whitney for help, she was torn. On the one hand, she wanted to get as far away as possible from this annoyingly gorgeous man, who insisted on flirting with her. On the other, how could she refuse to help when Luke was obviously struggling to bring up his adorable baby son?

Daddy Boom—*Who says bachelors and babies don't mix?*